THE BALTIC TRIANGLE

To Pam & Roger
with very very
Best wishes.

Neil C...

1. 12. 1C

THE BALTIC TRIANGLE

Nicholas Clark

ISBN 978 0 9553680 5 9

Printed and bound in Great Britain by Booksprint

You don't choose your family.
They are God's gift to you, as you are to them.
Thank you for my Gift.
Dad

Prologue

Jack Malaney had never known it so cold. It had taken him the better part of five years to become accustomed to the frigid conditions on board the MV Tongario, the mother ship to a large Russian Trawler fleet. The cold that they were experiencing at that moment was worse than anything that the weather-hardened crew had ever encountered before. The temperature gauge beside the water-tight door to the engine room had frosted over. A stiff Northerly had set in over a week ago and it blasted the coast of Halifax, Canada, day and night, ever since. The cold air froze everything that it came in contact with—instruments, doors, provisions and human beings. Jack ran his gloved hand across the glass face of the gauge and then he moved his head closer in an effort to take a reading. The needle was visible for a fleeting moment before being cloaked once again as Jack's warm breath made contact with the cold glass. Jack mumbled a few obscenities under his breath. He couldn't be certain of the exact reading but it was pointing far enough to the left and downwards for him to work out that it was well below freezing.

Jack pulled down hard on the handle of the engine room door and without even trying the door to check the resistance he threw his right shoulder against it. The door flew open and Jack entered the room. The difference in temperature between the engine room and the rest of the frozen ship was great and the skin on his face began to tingle as it quickly warmed up. The three men under his command, all Russian and all perpetually looking serious whenever Jack was around, turned to face him as he entered the room. They wore looks of annoyance that verged on anger—silently screaming at him to shut the damn door! Jack paused for a few moments before closing the door. It was never a good idea to jump whenever the Russians wanted him to—he would close the door on his terms and in his own good time. Роберт (Robert) was the most competent member of Jack's team. Jack called him Robert. Jack could never quite tell just how happy Роберт was with being renamed as the man looked angry all of the time—when they were eating; when they were playing poker; when they were drinking vodka—angry and depressed.

Jack had left Robert to work on one of the main water pumps that had come to a grinding halt with the terrible sound of metal scraping against metal, earlier that day. The pump removed the water that pooled at the lowest point of the ship and drove it out into the sea through an opening just above the ship's winter Plimsoll line. Jack feared that part of the outlet pipe had frozen solid but Robert insisted, in fewer than ten words, that the problem was located inside the pump itself.

"I fix," Robert had growled, before pushing Jack gently to one side.

Jack knew better than to argue with the Russian once his mind had been set on a particular course. Jack moved carefully across the oil and grease stained metal floor to check on Robert's progress. Robert's hands were covered with oil and the rag that he was using to wipe the metal parts before examining them was completely saturated in thick, black ooze. Robert was sucking slowly on a lit cigarette, the ash from which had almost reached the point where it could no longer support its own weight.

"Any luck?" Jack asked, as he towered over Robert who was sitting on a small wooden crate with the disassembled pump laid out before him.

The ash on the end of Robert's cigarette finally broke free and tumbled towards the pump as he turned to face Jack.

"Pump is fine. Pipe frozen," he said, simply.

Jack nodded his head. There was no point in saying to the Russian that he told him so. To do so would be asking for trouble. *You fix damn pipe yourself*, or some similar rebuke would be the only response. Jack struggled to suppress a grin. Any momentary pleasure Jack derived from being right soon vanished as he focused on what would happen next. The Russians were a hardy breed but they were by no means stupid. If the outlet pipe was indeed frozen then it would be left to Jack to sort the problem out. Jack quickly calculated in his head how long he could put the job off before the boat began to sink. It would take a good few weeks—weather permitting.

Rostislav and Ruslan, the other two members of his team, were sitting in front of one of the main engines. They didn't move when he entered the room—he loved that about his Russian team—there was no attempt to look busy just because the boss was around. The ship had power; everything was as it should be and so all that was left for the men to do was to keep themselves warm in whatever way they could. They were due to deliver fuel oil to two of the trawlers later that day and when that moment arrived they would all be out in the cold. Had the delivery been made in the middle of the summer it would only have taken two of them—one to oversee the oil as it was shipped to the trawler and one to manage the pump from the engine room. In the middle of the icy conditions it was not reasonable, or even possible, to leave one man out on the deck of the ship for too long as he checked on the progress of the delivery. They took it in turns. One would stay with the pipeline for ten minutes before the next member of the team came along to relieve him and so on, until they were all chilled to the bone, but no one man would be over exposed. Jack could have made his subordinates do all the work, but he knew that by leading by example the Russians would tolerate his presence. The fact that Jack was Scottish also helped as there was no chance that his team would have taken orders from an Englishman, or worse still, an American.

Jack smiled at the two comrades as they sat by the engine. The men returned smiles of their own—slight and half-hearted, but it was enough to indicate to Jack that they were happy for him to join them. He sat beside his two subordinates and mulled over the choice he would soon have to make—which of them would brave the cold first. Jack got lost in his own thoughts while his two Russian associates tentatively chatted to one another. There weren't many times when he regretted the decision he had made to take up his current position as chief engineer. The money was good; he got to see a bit of the world; and it was a chance for him to get away from his old life and be someone new, someone important. Life back home in Glasgow had been bleak. The employment situation was as bad as he could remember and crime was on the rise—a heavy, choking cloud of desperation had descended over the city and Jack believed that if he didn't escape it he would end up trapped and unhappy in the place he had once so warmly called home. Even the most poorly heated home in the worst maintained tenement building was warmer than life on board a boat in the middle of a North Atlantic winter. He toyed with the idea of only working during the spring and summer months but with so much unemployment all over the world it wouldn't be hard for the company to replace him with a chief engineer who didn't mind working all the year round.

A short time later the door to the engine room opened with a terrible screeching sound. A runner from the bridge entered the room. In a coarse, guttural Russian tone he said simply, "It is time."

With that the runner left. The three Russians played dumb. They continued with what they had been doing before the runner entered the room. This was a clear sign to Jack that if he wanted them to brave the cold up on deck then he would have to lead by example. Jack stood up.

"I'll take the first shift," he announced. "Then Robert, then Rostislav and then Ruslan."

The men groaned quietly. Jack knew that they had no grounds to complain when he was offering to go first, but he also knew that just because they had no grounds to complain that didn't mean that they wouldn't complain. On top of the many layers of winter clothing that he was already wearing Jack pulled on a fur-lined, waterproof coat. He moved to the door and then turned to his men. After a short pause they got to their feet and they began to slowly make preparations for the transfer of the fuel.

The deck of the ship was so cold that Jack's body began to feel pain from the moment that he stepped onto it. The wind had picked up strength and a snow shower was clouding his vision. He strained to catch a glimpse of the trawler that had pulled up beside their boat.

"Crazy Russians," he moaned to no one in particular.

The trawler rose and fell on the heavy seas. So much so that when the mother ship was falling into a trough and the trawler rising into a crest, the rigging from the fishing vessel was clearly visible. Jack looked across sympathetically at his counterpart on the trawler. All Jack had to do was brave the cold long enough to extend the fuel line across to the trawler. The man on the trawler had to complete the manoeuvre by feeding the pipeline into a relatively small opening in the fuel tank—with numb hands and thick gloves, this was a particularly frustrating process. On one occasion a Ukrainian fisherman had got so frustrated by the lack of dexterity afforded to him by his gloves that he took one of them off. He lost two fingers to frostbite, and his job into the bargain—it was a ruthless business and there were simply too many able bodied men willing and able to do the work for the skipper to accommodate a man with a handicap. Sentimentality was a concept that was alien to most commanders.

Jack moved across to the pumping station. He engaged the pump mechanism located in the engine room by turning a key, and then he readied himself by grabbing hold of the lever that controlled the speed and pressure of the fuel pump.

All he needed now was a signal that the man on the trawler was ready and Jack's part in this whole hellish process would be nearly over. Jack clapped his gloved hands together a few times—it was an entirely pointless exercise but it somehow reassured his body that he was aware of the cold and that he would do all he could to keep it at bay—his body was no fool.

On the high seas, even when re-running well rehearsed procedures, the angry water had a way of making human beings look small and foolish. The accident was no one's fault, but that did nothing to alleviate the severity of the consequences. The crewman from the trawler finally secured the heavy metal ring on the end of the delivery hose to the fuel tank. He signalled to Jack to begin pumping. Satisfied that everything was now in place, the crewman moved to the side of his boat where he lit a cigarette. Russians were crazy, but even they didn't smoke next to the fuel tank, even though fuel oil was notoriously difficult to ignite. Jack was increasing the power to the pump when it happened. Two large waves hit both vessels simultaneously. One wave caused the mother ship to heal to the left and the other wave caused the trawler to heal to the right. Jack almost lost his balance. The force of the motion put the fuel line connecting both vessels under great strain. Jack quickly moved to disengage the pump. As the motor driving the pump came to a stop the fuel line pulled free from the trawler and the heavy metal cap flew through the air like a missile. The trawler man didn't stand a chance. The end of the fuel line hit him on the back sending him over the low railing which ran along the section of the boat where he was standing. Jack dashed forward to the side of the ship and he looked down into the churning sea beneath him. It was like looking into a black, bubbling soup. Small speckles of light from the two vessels reflected off the water, hinting at what lay below but never quite providing Jack's eyes with enough information for him to make a decisive move.

"Man overboard," he yelled, across to the trawler. "Man overboard!"

It was no use. No one on the trawler could hear his cries. By the time the next member of the trawler crew came along to relieve the man in the sea it would be too late. Jack's mind raced in all kinds of directions. He had to act fast but there was no course of action open to him that didn't include a significant amount of danger to himself. The cold, rational part of his brain told him that the unfortunate sailor was already gone and that there was no point in turning one tragedy into two tragedies. The sentimental part of his brain brought images of his crewmates and pictures of their families to the front of his mind. The man in the water could have been married, he could have had a family—he was Russian after all, and they lived for their families. Jack knew what the loss of their main source of income would be to those he left behind—they would be out on the street— hungry, cold and forgotten.

In less than a minute, first Rostislav and then Ruslan arrived beside Jack at the side of the ship.

"We have to save him," Jack said.

The Russians looked at him as if he had gone mad. They knew as well as Jack did that the man was as good as dead.

"For god's sake, help me," Jack snapped. "I am not asking you to jump in to save him. Just get me a rope and a life jacket."

The men paused for a moment. They knew that their Scottish boss had an odd sense of humour and they couldn't be quite certain if this was just another manifestation of that peculiar character trait. He was serious. The men moved away from Jack and for once they hurried to carry out his orders.

Jack continued to strain his eyes in an effort to glimpse any sign of the lost soul. Then he saw it. Bobbing up and down on top of the murky water like a lazy seal on a hot summer's day—the trawler man's body, face down in the water. Rostislav and Ruslan returned. Ruslan was carrying a long, thick rope, but Rostislav was ominously empty handed.

"Life jacket?" quizzed Jack.

"None," Rostislav replied stoically.

"There are some in storage," Ruslan said.

Typical Soviet thinking, though Jack. Give the people what they need just don't make it too easy for them. It would never do if something was too easy—that is the Western way of thinking. Jack calculated that it would take them at least ten minutes to get to the correct storage compartment and back again—longer if the quartermaster had the lifejackets locked away—by this time of the day the quartermaster, a short, heavy man in his mid-fifties, was normally sleeping off the bottle of vodka he had for breakfast.

Jack secured one end of the rope to a sturdy, rust covered upright of the rail—again the thick gloves hindered his progress. His bewildered crewmates looked on with horror as Jack lashed the rope around his own waist, leaving a six foot length which he fashioned into a loop, secured with a stout double knot.

"A little help here lads," he said as he began to climb over the rail.

Rostislav and Ruslan knew that there was no reasoning with Jack and so they moved to help him over the rail. Jack faced his boat as the two men held onto the rope. The makeshift abseiling equipment was frightening, but that was nothing compared to the thought which flashed into Jack's mind as he began the descent towards the angry water—what if his two crewmates took this opportunity to rid themselves of him once and for all? This thought was soon replaced by the reality of what he was doing as he neared the thundering roar of the water as it rose and fell against the sides of the two vessels. The icy water got closer and closer. One good soaking and at the very least he would spend the next couple of weeks in sickbay.

"Down! Lower!" he yelled. The rope moved less than a foot each time he yelled. Jack may have been caught up in the excitement of the rescue to the extent that he was oblivious to most of the dangers surrounding him, but his crewmates were not—they didn't want to have to explain to their captain why they no longer had a chief engineer.

Jack looked up at the trawler when he was a few feet away from the man in the water. Three members of the crew were watching the action anxiously. It should have been one of them dangling precariously on the end of the rope, Jack thought. Some spray hit him on the face—a warning to get this over with.

"Lower," he yelled again.

Jack sized the situation beneath him for a moment but try as he might he could not see anyway to get the rope around the man other than Jack himself, or at least part of him, entering the water.

"Lower!" he called.

Jack's legs entered the water. The pain from the cold hit him like broken glass.

"Lower!"

This time down to his knees. His body trembling. His mind searching for a way to override his crazy actions.

"Lower!"

Into his waist. He worked quickly to loop the rope around the man. His hands and arms began to stiffen as the cold water penetrated his protective clothing. Rostislav and Ruslan had been joined by four other crewmen by the time Jack had fixed the rope to the dying seaman.

"Bring us up!" Jack called.

"Bring..."

Before he called for a second time his crewmates were pulling them up out of the water at a blissfully fast rate and before he had time to dwell too much on his body as it went into shock, they were being pulled up over the railing and onto the deck. Jack began to feel sleepy. The next thing he recalled was the ship doctor towering over him in sickbay.

"Bloody fool," snarled the doctor. "I expected better from you, Jack."

Jack was confused for a moment. There was very little feeling in the lower half of his body. This alarmed him greatly. He tried moving his legs. Nothing happened.

"Doctor, my legs. I can't move them."

"Aye," sighed the doctor. "Now he worries about his legs."

The doctor placed a reassuring hand on Jack's left leg.

"I have given you something for the pain. You will feel them again soon enough. You are a lucky man. There is only superficial damage to the skin. Sure, there will be some pain, but not enough to keep you off work I'm afraid."

The doctor smiled at Jack.

Jack smiled back but he still felt uneasy. It was as if the doctor was keeping something from him. Something very important. If finally came to him.

"How is the other man?" Jack asked.

The doctor shook his head.

"He is alive. In a few hours he may wish he wasn't, but for now, he's alive."

The doctor left Jack to recover. The doctor had a dry personality but there was something about the lack of emotion in what he said that gave Jack the impression that he was very serious—saving the man's life may not have been in his best interests. It was a moment in which Jack should have felt pride and joy, but as it happened, he couldn't help but feel dejected and apprehensive. After an hour, Jack fell asleep. It was an uneasy, restless slumber, troubled by consequences that he had not yet fully considered.

1

Daybreak

Jack awoke early the next morning. He was in a bed across from the sailor he had saved the previous evening. He didn't know if any of the man's shipmates had come aboard to visit the sailor. He didn't know if any of his own crewmates had paid him a visit while he was asleep. The feeling had returned to his legs. The pain was mild. He swung his legs onto the side on the bed and cautiously he put his feet on the floor. Relief pulsed through his body when his legs took the full weight of his body with ease. He carefully made his way across the room to where the still unconscious trawler man was lying. He was bandaged from head to toe. A saline drip was slowly feeding fluid into a vein in his arm. This was the most primitive kind of intensive care. The weather must have been bad the night before or they would have had him airlifted to shore.

Jack reached out and gently squeezed the man's left arm. There was no reaction. He squeezed a little harder. Still nothing. The doctor was right. He had saved his life only to prolong his death. If he had to do it over again, he asked himself, would he have done anything differently? As he looked at the lifeless bundle of rags lying on the bed in front of him, he still answered yes.

"He will be fine," said a voice, from behind him.

The voice startled Jack. He spun round to face the source. The woman standing by the doorway to the sickbay was not what he had been expecting. It wasn't unusual for the Russians to have female commanders on their ships, but what was unusual about this female captain was just how beautiful she was. The other women he had met out at sea looked every inch as though out at sea was exactly where they belonged. This woman was very different. She was six foot tall, with blond hair so light that it verged on being white. Her hair flowed effortlessly over her shoulders and down her back. Her deep blue eyes seemed perfectly set against the pale complexion of her skin. She looked like the perfect ice queen, but her voice was warm and comforting, like a long drink of whiskey on a cold winter's night. Jack's mouth opened slightly as he struggled to form a sentence which wasn't complete gibberish.

"I am Captain Alyona Ulyana, and on behalf of myself and my crew I would like to thank you for saving the life of our comrade. We owe you a great debt of gratitude."

Jack remained silent.

"What is the matter, crewman?" Alyona continued. "You do not look at all happy."

"Aye Captain, it's not that. I just don't know if I did the right thing."

The Captain looked confused for a moment.

"Why do you say this, crewman?"

"Malaney. Jack Malaney. Our doctor reckons that he will be in such bad shape when he finally comes round that it might have been better if we had left him to die."

The Captain smiled.

"Russian doctors are not known for their over enthusiastic prognoses. He will be fine. He is being evacuated to the shore today and he will be back in his homeland in a few days. Once he gets the sweet Russian air in his lungs he will make a remarkable recovery. Don't you worry about him."

She smiled again. Her words lifted Jack's spirits and he gave her a smile in return.

"We are all so grateful and I insist that you join me this evening at my table for some dinner. My crew want to thank you. I want to thank you."

"I will have to ask my Captain for permission, but..."

"Already done," she interrupted. "I have arranged for transportation. I will see you at 1800 hours."

She turned on her heal and left before Jack had a chance to protest. This was a woman who knew what she wanted and she was damn sure she was going to get her own way, one way or the other. Jack understood why she was in command of her own ship.

Captain Ulyana's ship was one of the most modern trawlers he had been on. By Jack's estimation the ship couldn't have been any more than a couple of years old. The paintwork was starting to show a bit of weathering and there was the odd spot of rust here and there, but the general condition of the vessel was good. Jack smiled to himself—why did the woman captains always command the cleanest ships?

Two bearded crewmen escorted Jack through the ship. They didn't speak to him at all—they certainly didn't give him the impression that they were glad to see him—it was far from the hero's welcome that he had been expecting. Jack's next surprise came when he was ushered into the Captain's private quarters. The room was big for a trawler, and very comfortably furnished. There were paintings of frozen landscapes on the walls and two gas heaters roared fiercely at either side of a small dining table. Jack couldn't help but notice that the table was only set for two. Captain Ulyana was already seated. She was a proud woman and even though she had brought him onboard to thank him for saving the life of one of her crew, she was not going to break protocol by standing when he walked into the room—she was in command and he was just a crewman—she didn't stand for crewmen, ever.

"Jack, come in. Have a seat. You must be frozen? Close the door," she barked, and one of the men who had escorted Jack to the Captain's room pulled the door closed, leaving Jack and the Captain alone in the room.

As Jack approached her his nostrils were filled with the delicate notes of fresh flowers coming from her perfume. He hadn't smelled anything like that since the last time he was home in Scotland. He liked it, the smell of a woman. She was wearing a black, sleeveless dress—a brave choice considering the weather conditions, Jack thought. She smiled warmly and extended a hand, inviting him to take a seat across from her, which he did, if somewhat awkwardly.

"I will introduce you to my men later," she began. "I prefer to eat on my own, but for you I will make an exception. You see, my crew, as loyal and hard working as they are, do smell like feet all of the time. And if it's not feet, then they smell of oil. I have concluded that neither of these two odours is conducive to enjoying a good meal."

Jack smiled. He had showered before he left the ship but it was a cold, half-hearted attempt at cleaning himself and as he sat there in the warm room he felt certain that he could smell oil rising from his body.

"I know what you mean," he said, sheepishly.

"I am afraid that the food onboard is functional rather than delectable, but our cook is a master at turning even the simplest of fare into something wonderful. He has prepared some thick steaks with fried potato."

"Sounds wonderful. We haven't had a good steak in ages."

She smiled again.

"I didn't say that he had prepared a good steak."

Jack smiled back.

"So Jack, before the food comes, answer me this. What makes a man risk his own life to save the life of a stranger?"

"I don't know," Jack explained. "I just saw him lying there in the water and I knew that I had to do something to help him. He might have a family waiting for him back home. A wife. Children. It was just the right thing to do."

"Wonderful, Jack. The right thing to do. I like that."

"I'm sure any member of your crew would have done the same thing had they been in my position."

She let slip a loud laugh.

"Hardly Jack. They would have said that the bloody fool deserved everything that he got and left him to drown. A boat is a dangerous place and if you are not prepared to look out for yourself then you can't expect anyone else to risk their life to look out for you."

"I don't think so," Jack continued. "It is easy for any of us to say words like that but when we are face to face with the actual choice of whether or not to save the life of a fellow human being; I think you'll find that most people would do what I did. It's not heroic, it's just human."

"If you say so, Jack. Perhaps you should spend a little time in the Soviet Union, and then you will get a true sense of the value of a human life."

Jack knew that it was pointless arguing with her and so he let the matter drop. After a few minutes the cook came into the room, set down their meals in front of them and then he left.

"Eat up Jack," she commanded. "It will be like ice in no time at all."

He did as she commanded. The steak was tender, a little too rare for his liking, but enjoyable nevertheless. They didn't speak a word the entire time they were eating. This was something that he had noticed about the Russians—mealtimes were not a time for chitchat—it was almost as if they were on their guard, fearing that someone might swoop in at any moment to remove the food from their plates. Captain Ulyana cleared her plate faster than any woman he had ever met. He had tried to keep up with her but it was no use, he simply couldn't put the food away fast enough. She waited politely for him to finish. She looked at him hungrily as he continued to eat and then smiled warmly when he finally set the knife and fork down on the empty plate.

"Good?" she asked.

"Better than good. It was excellent."

"I am glad you approved. I will pass your compliments along to the cook."

"Please do."

"So Jack, before I bring you out to meet your adoring fans, tell me a little about yourself. I know you are Scottish and I know that you are very brave, or very stupid, depending on who you talk to, but what else do I need to know about the man? How did you end up out here in the middle of nowhere working with a Russian crew?"

"Money, plain and simple. There is very little work back home."

"Really? I always imagined Britain to be much like America. Lots of fat people with very little to do and all the time in the world to do it in."

"I'm afraid not. There are plenty of people chasing their own tails trying to make a living and plenty of others just longing for the chance to work. But fat and lazy? If only."

"Good for you Jack. I am glad that you have made something of your life. I am glad that you are able to make some money to send back home to your family. Do you have a wife? Children?"

"No wife and no children that I know of."

She laughed again.

"So you are a hot blooded male then, Jack?"

"Not as hot blooded as I'd like to be, but I can but try."

She laughed again.

For a few moments there was silence. When she began to speak again there was slight change to her tone of voice—it was suddenly a little more serious.

"I have been to Scotland, Jack," she began. "Well, I have been off the coast of Scotland, to be more correct. Mmm... let me see. I am not so familiar with your coastline. It was close to Glasgow. In fact I got into a bit of trouble in those waters."

"What happened?"

"It was near Dunoon. I had dropped anchor and we were going to take a few days rest. Your navy came along after a few hours and they boarded my vessel. They searched it from top to bottom and then they moved us along. We must have been in waters where we were not supposed to be. A military area, or something?"

Her words hit Jack like a club to the face. Suddenly everything started to make sense. None of the crew that he had met, or any of his own crew, were in the least bit interested in Jack saving the man's life, yet she was. More than that, she was much too impressed. Now he knew why. The American nuclear submarine fleet often lay off Dunoon. She hadn't brought him onto her ship in order to thank him, she had brought him onto her ship to gently, subtly, pump him for information. He was not about to be used by her, no matter how charming she was.

"Military area?" Jack replied, with a quizzical expression on his face. "I have been fishing in those waters many times. I wasn't aware that there were any restrictions."

Her expression changed suddenly. Although her tone remained calm and amiable, her eyes were filled with anger. She knew that he was lying.

"I am surprised that you are not aware of the restrictions. Perhaps they only apply to foreign vessels? Or maybe it is only Soviet vessels that are stopped?"

"It could be," Jack said, simply.

Her plan was now in tatters. She stood up.

"I am sure that you want to get back to your ship," she said.

Jack knew that she was after information and that when they set their minds to a task Russians could be incredibly tenacious, and so he took the opportunity to get away while he still could. There was no further talk of meeting with her crew. There was no mention of his new hero status. The two men who had escorted him to the Captain's quarters were waiting outside the door to ensure that he made it safely back to his own ship.

The events gave Jack a lot to think about. He had a friend working on the police force back home and when he was on shore leave a few days later he made contact with him—it was too risky to try to make contact from his ship, not if the Russians were spying on him, which he now believed they were.

His friend, Harry Kirker was very interested in what Jack had to say and he told him to leave the matter with him. Three days later Harry made contact with Jack. The conversation was short and quite cryptic, but Harry promised to tell him everything once he was back home in Scotland. Jack had to spend another two weeks on the ship before it was time to return home. They were two of the most uncomfortable weeks of his life. His shipmates were even more hostile than usual and at any moment he felt that he could be dragged off and interrogated. That never happened. And so Jack returned to Scotland. When he got back home his life would never be the same again.

2

The Call of Duty

The bitter cold of the North Atlantic was replaced by the more familiar and tolerable cold of Glasgow. January was always the gloomiest month in the city as the celebrations and fun of the Christmas holidays gave way to the drudgery and complexity of returning to work in the middle of a Scottish winter. Heavy snowfalls from the middle of December had initially left the city's population feeling very festive, but as the snow turned grey and dirty, then from slush to ice, the novelty had well and truly wore off. All eyes looked to spring but Mother Nature hadn't quite finished testing the good people of the city quite yet.

As Jack walked along Queen Street towards George Square, the sense that the partying and joy of the holidays was at an end was all too apparent—from the January Sales signs in shop windows, to the emptiness and boredom in the eyes of those whom he passed on the streets. His paced slowed as he approached a couple in their early thirties having a row with a council worker—the girl had slipped on an icy footpath and the young man was holding the unfortunate council worker responsible, even though he was only truly guilty of being in the wrong place at the wrong time. The worker tried to explain that salting the footpath was not his job but the irate young man was having none of it. Jack felt that the argument was about to turn physical but as he got closer he could hear the man from the council giving the young man a telephone number—had the city really changed that much since he had gone? Were arguments now settled through diplomacy and reason. He certainly hoped not as it would make a Friday night at the pub a lot less entertaining.

He loved Christmas and New Year in the city but the money that he had been offered to remain on the boat over the holidays was simply too good to turn down. The Russians were an atheist nation by decree of their government, but in reality they were one of the most religious people that he had ever encountered, second only to the Irish. The early years of Communism had been hard on religion in the Russian states but as time went by and the corrupt leadership quickly set themselves up as the new aristocracy, the decision to allow the people to worship their God was a very pragmatic concession—they were never going to attain the utopia that they had been promised in this life, so at the very least they could dream of a better afterlife. Christmas meant a lot to the Russians and the company had great difficulties keeping their vessels crewed during the festive period. They offered double pay for any man willing to keep the boats at sea.

George Square was one of his favourite parts of the city. The City Chambers in particular he found very pleasing on the eye and they gave a sense that Glasgow was an important city in its own right rather than just a Northerly outpost of the British Empire. He spent several minutes in the Square simply looking at the buildings and casually observing as people walked past—everyone in a hurry, everyone rushing to their next sanctuary from the biting cold. Sentimentality aside, he would not have been in the Square had there not been a very good reason for him to be there, and just because he liked the place that would not have been enough of a motivation to bring him out of the warmth of the hotel on that day. Jack had to meet with Harry Kirker at the Strathclyde Police Authority next to George Square and so that morning he set out a little earlier so that he could spend a little time just looking around and recalling some of the happier times that he had spent in that part of the city. As the time of his appointment with Harry approached Jack set in his mind to take in a bit more of the city when he was finished—he had never once thought that he would miss the city quite as much as he did when he was on the boat. The grass wasn't always greener after all, but the money certainly was.

He loved government-run buildings such as the Police Authority for one simple reason—they were always really warm—regardless of the cutbacks being imposed on government bodies, no one ever went as far as turning the heat down a little. A far cry from the Baltic conditions felt in some of the struggling businesses across the city—it was almost as if the health of a company or shop could be judged by how warm the premises were.

A heavy, bald, uniformed policeman looked over the top of his half spectacles at Jack when he entered the Police Authority building. The policeman fussed over some papers sitting on the desk in front of him as Jack approached—more likely to be betting slips rather than arrest sheets, Jack thought. A mug of tea sat next to a small, shiny bell that looked as if it hadn't been used very often. The policeman lifted the mug and took a loud sip of tea. He continued to hold the mug in an effort to set the tone—no matter how urgent Jack thought his business was, this man was not going to be rushed, Jack thought.

"Jack Malaney?" the policeman asked, much to Jack's surprise.

"Yes," he replied, simply.

"Inspector Kirker is expecting you. If you could follow me?"

The policeman set the mug of tea down carefully on the desk and then he stepped out from behind his desk and he began to walk along the corridor towards the stairs. Jack quickly followed. He caught up with the policeman at the bottom of the stairs.

"Inspector Kirker is it? God, it seems like no time at all since he was dirty wee Harry Kirker, running along the backstreets of Glasgow in short trousers," Jack said to the policeman, as they moved up the stairs.

The policeman smiled.

"Nothing has changed," the policeman remarked. "Except of course, he is an inspector now."

They walked along the first floor corridor until they reached a room at the end. The policeman went through the doorway and Jack followed him. There was a woman sitting behind a desk. She flashed a smile at the policeman. Her accent was not local to Glasgow—it sounded a lot more Northern, Jack thought, perhaps even from one of the islands?

"And what brings you up to the corridor of power today?" the woman asked, to her colleague.

"Jack Malaney here has an appointment with the inspector. Inspector Short Trousers, as he's soon to be known as," said the policeman.

The receptionist looked confused.

"I'll tell you later dear," said the policeman.

The woman stood up.

"I'll just pop my head round the door and check if you can go on through," she said.

The secretary moved to a door behind where she had been sitting and cautiously opened it. Jack smiled—she literally popped her head around the doorway.

"Jack Malaney is here," she said.

She returned to her desk and sat down before relaying the response from the inspector.

"You can go right on through," she said.

"Nice to meet you sir," the policeman said, before walking out through the doorway and back down the corridor.

Jack nodded to the policeman as he left. He then walked around the side of the receptionist's desk and on into Harry's office. Jack had been ready to let fly with a long sentence that was heavily peppered with friendly obscenities when he greeted Harry, but the fact that Harry was not alone scuppered that plan.

Harry got up from behind his desk and he walked around to shake Jack's hand. He was smiling widely and Jack smiled back.

"Jack, you have no idea how good it is to see you. We have so much catching up to do," Harry said.

"So it would seem, Inspector," Jack replied. "When the hell did that happen? And has the force really run out of competent officers to promote?"

"Aye, they are making anyone an officer these days. No one wants to do the job. Too much like hard work."

"Hard work Harry? You are talking to man coming off a four month stint on board a stinking Russian ship in the freezing Atlantic. You wouldn't know hard work if it jumped up and bit you on the arse."

"You always were a good bullshitter, Jack. Just remember who you are talking to. Four month pleasure cruise, more like. You found yourself a nice wee warm nest somewhere and slept the time away."

Harry stood to one side so that Jack could move past him.

"Take a seat Jack. The gentleman sitting ominously behind my desk is Officer Reilly. He has come all the way from London just to meet with you. He is one of her Majesty's spooks."

Jack reached across the desk and shook Reilly's hand.

"And why do you need to talk to me?" Jack asked, with a hint of trepidation in his voice.

"Just a few things I'd like for you to consider," Reilly said, cryptically.

"Officer Reilly," Harry began, as he sat down. "Jack is what we north of the border like to call a dim wit. Your James Bond double talk is going to go right over his head if you aren't careful. Spit it out man, in words that even Jack can understand."

Reilly looked more than a little uncomfortable. It was obvious that he was not used to dealing with someone as straight shooting as Harry.

"As I was saying," Reilly continued. "We would like to make you an offer. We would like to know how you would feel about serving your country."

Harry and Jack exchanged slight grins.

"You want me to play for Scotland?" Jack asked, playfully. "It has always been a dream of mine to play for my country, but I don't know that my knees could stick the abuse. I could sit on the substitution bench and give the lads a wee pull out near the end of the match. Or maybe I could manage the squad? I couldn't be any worse than the clown they've got at the minute."

Reilly didn't know how to continue. He was not used to being mocked openly like this but as Jack was not on his payroll then there really wasn't a lot that he could do to force him to take what he was saying seriously. Reilly's frustration gave the two friends great pleasure and they struggled to contain their delight.

"Come on Jack, give the officer a break," Harry said. "Just because he's English, that's no reason for us to be rude. Officer Reilly would like you to spy on the Russians. He will tell you how important the job is and how you are protecting the very future of our way of life. He won't tell you just how dangerous it is. So, laying it on the line for you—would you be prepared to work as a spy, and if so, how much is it going to cost the government?"

Reilly looked genuinely horrified. He spluttered into action.

"I... I... It... The salary drawn by our spies is set by Whitehall and it is not open to negotiation."

"Bollocks to that," Harry snapped. "We waste money by the billions every year on defence. Are you telling me that the British government couldn't scrape together a little something extra for my mate here, by way of danger money?"

Reilly again looked completely stunned. This was not how the recruitment process was supposed to go. It was a well rehearsed, highly finessed procedure. It involved meetings in spacious parks or smoky pubs; it was a gradual movement towards trust being built and loyalty secured.

What it certainly was not, was a union style pay negotiation with two Scotsmen standing years of protocol on its head.

"I... There is a little bit of flexibility," Reilly conceded.

Harry nodded at Jack and smiled.

"See Jack, I knew he was holding out on you," Harry said.

"I can assure you, that is not the case," Reilly protested.

"Ah, come on officer," Harry said. "One minute the salary is fixed by Whitehall and the next minute it is open to negotiation."

"I just meant to say that..." Reilly began.

Harry cut across him. The tone of Harry's voice completely changed. Gone was any trace of joviality, replaced by a menacing tone of dark sincerity that caused Reilly to sit back in his seat.

"Here is the bottom line, Officer Reilly. You are asking one of my oldest and dearest friends to put his life on the line for your organisation. Let's put to one side the Queen and Country spiel. If he accepts your offer you will give him everything that is owed to him. Full salary; danger money; the works. You will put in place a good pension plan for him, and, God forbid, should he end up in some Russian prison, or worse, you have a legal arrangement in place that his salary will continue. It will be paid to his mother, and when she is no longer with us, it will be sent to his brother or sister, as Jack sees fit. If you can't agree to these terms then you can take your arse to the station down the road and piss off back to London. How does that sound to you?"

Reilly regained his composure.

"I am really not accustomed to dealing with a potential spy's agent," he said, sardonically.

"It is fortunate then that I don't give a damn what you are accustomed to. This is how it is going to be. Take it or leave it," Harry added.

Jack sat back in his seat and he enjoyed the show. He had never seen this side of Harry before and he understood now why he had reached such an important position at such a young age. He was spectacular.

Reilly stood up. It looked to all the world that he was about to walk out in a strunt.

"I will have all the necessary papers drawn up," Reilly said.

"I'll be wanting to have a wee gander at those," Harry returned.

"Inspector Kirker, do you understand what a Secret Service is?" Reilly asked.

"Aye, as it happens. A bunch of public schoolboys pissing around with real people's lives."

"The papers will be drawn up. Mr Malaney can confirm that all of your demands have been included in his terms of employment. And that's all Mr Malaney will confirm. I will be in touch."

With that said Reilly left the office. Harry started grinning like the cheeky schoolboy that Jack knew from his childhood.

"Harry, what the hell just happened?" Jack asked.

"I just got you a job as the next Scottish James Bond. It's about time that we had another one. Though you aren't exactly Sean Connery."

All through his childhood Jack had been in all kinds of trouble. The only constant in all of this bother was Harry. Now as adults Harry was settling back into his old role. As Jack settled back into a long conversation with his oldest friend, the events that had just transpired seemed more like a comical dream. The reality of that dream was soon to manifest in Jack's world. All thoughts of sightseeing were now gone from his mind.

3

At Your Service

The Best Western Hotel near the city centre was the place that Jack chose to call home when he was back in Scotland. He told the family that he didn't want to be a bother to his elderly mother, but in reality, as much as he loved them, the six nieces and four nephews that his brother and sister had spawned between them were more fun and excitement than Jack could handle on a daily basis. The hotel was his refuge, his sanctuary, his home away from home. When he was a teenager he admired the Best Western—it was just the kind of town house that he would buy one day when he made his fortune. Renting a room for a few weeks at a time, three or four times a year, was as close as he was likely to get to fulfill that boyhood dream.

It was the last Saturday in January. He was due to return to the ship in eight days time and he hadn't heard anything more about his new job working as a British secret agent. The more he thought about it the more he believed it to have been an elaborate hoax set up and executed by his old friend Harry Kirker. The whole thing was simply too bloody ridiculous. If they really did want him to be a spy then there wasn't exactly a lot of time left to train before he returned to the boat.

His answer came when he got out of bed just before ten that morning. Sitting in his room without a care in the world, as if that kind of behaviour was the most normal thing in the world, was Officer Reilly.

"What the hell do you think you are doing?" Jack snapped.

"Don't be alarmed Jack. You don't mind if I call you Jack?"

"I don't mind what you call me, just as long as you call me first from the other side of that door. I could have killed you!"

"Hardly Jack," Reilly replied, smugly.

"Is that right big man? Your special forces training might impress the Ruskies, but it's no match for a good old fashioned Glasgow kiss."

"As you wish Jack. As I was trying to explain, my presence should not be mistaken as being in any way sinister. I couldn't very well have waited out in thecorridor for you to wake up. And as you were sleeping soundly I didn't think it proper to wake you. Once you are on the payroll I will not be quite so considerate."

"Sinister, well maybe not, but it is definitely creepy."

Jack got dressed. Reilly turned to face in the other direction as Jack got ready. It was a bazaar experience. Reilly had a way with him that exuded menace by virtue of the fact that he was suspiciously quiet when he ought to be speaking and incomprehensively vocal when he ought to be keeping his mouth shut. In short, the man made Jack's skin crawl. If the new job entailed working closely under Reilly then he set in his mind to respectfully decline the offer.

"So Mr Reilly, what exactly would you have me do? I mean, I am working on a Russian supply vessel. It isn't exactly at the heart of the Soviet nuclear missile program."

"That's the thing Jack. We don't exactly know what is or what is not at the heart of the Soviet nuclear missile program. It is not beyond the realms of possibility that there is a fleet of nuclear powered, nuclear armed submarines off the coast of the United States and the United Kingdom. We have chased three out of the Irish Sea in the last year alone."

Jack was genuinely surprised by what he was hearing. If that was the case and Russia was of a mind to destroy the UK, then there wasn't a hell of a lot that we could do about it, Jack thought.

"The nuclear power means that they can in theory stay out at sea for years at a time. However, the boats are manned by human beings and even Russian sailors need food and other provisions. They can get them by going back into Soviet ports, but if they do that they know that there is a risk we will tag them. Once we know where they are it is much easier to keep track of them. It is much more likely that the submarines stay at sea and that they get supplies and fresh crews brought to them."

"Surely they would have to surface in order to do that," Jack interrupted.

"There is a risk of being spotted but the vastness of the Atlantic affords them much greater cover than a Russian port. We did have a bit of luck at around this time last year when the Canadian Coast Guard boarded a trawler off the coast of Newfoundland. The boat had more than three times the normal crew compliment for a ship of its size and even though they had been at sea for three weeks, they hadn't caught a single fish. They were either the most unlucky fishermen in history or they were a Russian submarine crew, just off one of the boats or ready to board one of them. And that is where you come in. Your vessel services several trawlers. We need you to keep an eye out for any suspicious behaviour."

"Such as?"

"The trawlers offload their catch to your vessel to be placed into cold storage?"

"That's true," Jack said.

"Watch for boats heading out to sea and returning empty handed, like our friends from last year. If we know which trawlers are involved in the practice then we stand a good chance of marking at least some of the Russian nuclear submarine fleet."

"Forgive my ignorance, but what good would that do? I mean, unless you sink them now, surely there wouldn't be time to act in the event of a nuclear attack?"

"We, and the Americans have a fleet of hunter-destroyer submarines. When we tag a Russian sub we have one of our hunter-destroyers shadow it. They play cat and mouse up and down the Eastern Seaboard of the US and Canada. In the event of an attack the destroyers will be instructed to sink the Russian subs. It could very well make the difference between our survival and complete destruction. It may sound melodramatic, but that is how we view it."

"Surely the Russians have enough ICBM's to destroy the US and UK without the need for their submarine fleet?"

"True, but we have measures in place to deal with most of them. No, the real danger comes from those hidden missiles close to our shores. There is no chance of surface to air missile interception, or fighter interceptions, so close to their targets. That is why it is so important to have men like you out there providing us with intelligence."

Jack paced backwards and forwards across the room as he considered what he had been told. Reilly gave him space and time to think. The idea of helping his country survive a nuclear attack appealed to him. But on the downside, if the Russians thought for even a moment that he was spying on them then he would be sure to meet with a tragic, fatal accident. He had his own family to think about—it would completely devastate his mother. Also, it wasn't the kind of job he could accept one day, and then change his mind about a few days later. If he was in then he was in for good.

"You have to understand," Jack said, eventually. "This is a lot for me to take in. You know better than most what it is that you are asking of me. It is not just my personal safety that I have to think about. There is my family to consider."

"I completely understand Jack. I will leave you to make up your mind. I have business at the University of Glasgow. Could you meet my later outside the Kelvingrove Museum? At around three?" Reilly asked, with sincere expectation in his voice.

"I can do that," Jack replied.

Reilly shook Jack's hand and then he moved towards the entrance of the room. He glanced back at Jack before quietly slipping out into the corridor. Jack sat on the edge of the bed and he began the torturous process of trying to decide what to do next.

4

The Name's Malaney...

Jack stood outside the Kelvingrove Museum in the freezing cold waiting to meet with Reilly. He had lived in the city all his life but Jack had never been inside the museum. He hadn't been inside many of the City's museums. He had been standing patiently since five to three. At three fifteen he began to wonder if Reilly was going to show at all. He waited another five minutes and then he swore softly under his breath before walking away from the building. Anger rumbled inside his head—Reilly had been so insistent about meeting with him. Perhaps Harry Kirker had been correct in his assessment of Reilly and the organisation that he represented? They only existed to mess ordinary people like him around. It wouldn't have surprised Jack in the least if Reilly was watching him from the warmth of one of the nearby buildings and having a good laugh at his expense. The reality was a little different. Jack was merely yards into his retreat from the museum when a voice called out from behind him.

"Jack!"

Jack turned to face Reilly as he came running towards him. His face was flushed and sweat ran down his forehead and pooled under his eyes. This was not play acting. Reilly was out of breath when he finally came to a stop in front of Jack.

"A million apologies, old boy. I got caught up with a couple of old friends and time got away from me. I am sorry to have kept you waiting."

Jack looked at Reilly coldly, not only because his excuse

was so flimsy, but more so because of the over familiar way that he was talking to him. They were not friends, they would never be friends and he would rather have the creepy, stoic Reilly to this cheery version of himself that he was now presenting.

"No bother," Jack replied.

Reilly placed a hand on Jack's back and he gently pushed him in the direction of the museum.

"We can go inside," Reilly said.

"No mate," Jack protested. "The place is shut up. I've already tried to get in."

Reilly smiled. Although he didn't intend for it to appear that way, the smile was extremely smug, and it annoyed the hell out of Jack.

"I have arranged to be let in for a little while. Somewhere warm and quiet for us to have a little chat. We won't be disturbed. Follow me, there's a nice warm cup of tea waiting for us inside."

Jack was certain that the museum was empty, so exactly who did he call to arrange for them to be let inside? Although it was not late in the day the dark clouds and fading light meant that the lights in all of the surrounding buildings were on—the museum remained completely unlit. Reilly walked up to the front door with a confident bounce to his step. As he expected this to be a wasted journey, Jack followed at a slow pace behind. To Jack's surprise the door opened the first time Reilly tried it. Reilly caught sight of Jack's disbelief. The man simply couldn't help himself—another slight, smug grin, washed across his face.

"Don't worry Jack. There is nothing spy-related going on. A friend of mine is a professor of ancient history at the University. He got me into the museum outside of opening hours in the past and he was good enough to arrange for us to use the building today. He called across to the caretaker before I left his office."

Jack nodded his head. A friend of mine, he recalled, with

annoyance—a friend of mine from my Oxford days, no doubt. They went into the building. The caretaker was waiting for them. The caretaker was a tall, thin man with glasses.

"Welcome gents," said the caretaker. "There is a wee cup of tea waiting for you in the main reading room. If you need anything else, just give me a shout."

"Thank you," Reilly replied.

Reilly and Jack began to walk towards the main reading room as the caretaker locked the doors to the museum.

"Gents," called the caretaker. "I will be locking up in an hour. So unless your business here is a matter of national security, I would be grateful if you'd be ready to leave when I am."

Jack looked at Reilly with mild alarm on his face. Reilly smiled that same smug smile again.

"He's messing with you Jack," Reilly said.

Jack spoke in a low voice.

"National Security? A bit on the nose, don't you think?"

"Right on the nose, I'd say."

"He knows what we are up to?"

"Yes Jack, he knows exactly what we are up to. Andrew is one of us."

"One of us? A spy? Here?" Jack asked, with confusion.

"British universities are, and have been for many years, a hotbed for foreign agents. Andrew is only one of many counter intelligence officers working at the University here in the city. Most of the work carried out on new defence systems takes place at the universities. The secret services have been trying to get successive governments to take all classified research out of academia, as is the case in the US and Russia, but they always refused. It's all about power. The civil service would never go for it. The best we can do is put men like Andrew in place and hope for the best."

"In a museum?"

"Of course. This place and the library are where most meetings take place. Ideal for a covert conversation, wouldn't you say?"

Jack said nothing as he looked around the exhibits. It certainly wouldn't have been the ideal location if he wanted to have a secret meeting with another spy. They sat down at a table in the reading room. They were surrounded by high bookcases that were packed to overflowing with thick, scholarly works. The vast majority of the books looked old and well used. Reilly poured them both a cup of tea from a tall china teapot. Milk and sugar sat on a tray in containers which matched the teapot.

"So Jack. Now that you have had some time to think things over, what is your decision?" Reilly asked, with expectation in his voice.

Jack cleared his throat, took a sip of tea, and then he paused purposefully—he could be every bit as dramatic as Reilly when the mood took him.

"In principle, my answer is yes. I would like to know a bit more about what the job entails, and what I get paid. But yes, you can count me in."

Reilly smiled again. This time it was a smile of warmth—it was almost sincere.

"That is wonderful Jack. Your government and your country are in your debt."

Reilly reached into the inside pocket of his jacket and he pulled out a piece of folded paper which he slid across the table to Jack. Jack lifted the piece of paper and he opened it slowly. Jack's eyebrows lifted as he read the figure on the paper.

"Well Jack, is it acceptable?" asked Reilly.

There was a pause during which Jack contorted his face like a mechanic preparing to deliver some bad, costly news, to a customer.

"Mmm. One thing confuses me," Jack said.

"Yes?"

"How the hell does James Bond afford all those sports cars and his champagne lifestyle on that salary?"

Reilly smiled.

"All equipment is supplied in addition to the salary," Reilly explained.

"So the Aston Martin will be waiting for me back at my hotel?" Jack asked, with a grin.

"I've been working for the service for ten years and I'm still waiting on mine," said Reilly. "So Jack, can I count you in?"

Jack nodded his head, yes. Reilly smiled as he reached across the table and shook Jack's hand. It was a firm grip, but a weak handshake. Jack had been expecting as much.

"Welcome to the service," Reilly said, simply.

5

Very Basic Training

Jack's first day as a spy was not what he had been expecting. He was picked up outside his hotel by a guy in a Land Rover at seven that morning. It was still dark, and very cold. His driver, Michael, was a Geordie who had been with the service for five years. He was an ex-SAS man and he now worked as an instructor in hand-to-hand combat, small arms and explosives. There appeared to be no back doors to Michael as he answered each and every one of Jack's questions in a full and frank fashion, and there were points during those answers when Jack wished he had been a little more guarded and brief.

Their destination for the day was Galloway Forest Park. The 300 square miles of the park provided such a vast variety of territories that it was the primary training area for the service in the UK, according to Michael. His day was to mainly consist of two sessions on hand-to-hand combat, as this was most likely to be of benefit to him when he was back on his ship, should he get into trouble. The improvised weapons training session that Michael mentioned sounded intriguing until Michael explained that it was mainly concerned with using everyday objects to deadly affect—it didn't take much training to teach a man how to lamp someone with a wrench, or smash his face in with a brick, Jack thought.

The small arms training was part of the overall basic training program that every new recruit went through, but Michael explained that it would be too risky to send Jack back to his ship with a gun.

"Aye, they'll feed it to you if they catch you with a gun," Michael explained. "You will be rumbled as a spook straight away. They will have their own spies on your ship and you will be their main focus, as a foreigner. Have you ever gone back to your quarters to find stuff not quite where you thought you left it?"

"Eh, no. I can't say that I have."

Michael smiled. "Exactly, that's just how bloody good they are. But seriously, they will have been watching you like a hawk over the past few years and they will routinely search through your stuff. We certainly would. There is a good chance that your room is also bugged. All calls that you make from the ship will be recorded and analysed."

This revelation surprised Jack only a little. When one of his men used the communications room to call home they were always given privacy, but anytime he placed a call home, one of the communications officers always stayed with him "in case he needed help." Jack didn't like the idea of going back to the boat to spy without being armed — it might only be used in a last, desperate, pointless act of defence, but he would rather go down fighting, taking as many of the Reds with him as he possibly could. He pushed his case further.

"I could carry the weapon on me at all times. We wear heavy, bad-weather gear most of the time — they would never notice a concealed weapon."

"No good mate. You will not be wearing that gear all of the time," Michael explained.

"Like when I'm in the shower?"

"Yes."

"I could always take it in with me."

"And if they walk in when you are showering?"

"Not bloody likely!"

"If they suspected for one minute that you wear a spy, they would walk in when you were on the bog. They will be doing everything they can to prove that you are a spy, and believe me, it won't take much evidence for them to send you back to Mother Russia for some quiet time in a Siberian prison. It is your job, at all times, to prove them wrong. No mate, no gun. No gun and no radio."

"Then how the hell am I supposed to report back?"

"For the most part, you won't. You will wait until you are back home in the UK, and then you can identify the trawlers of interest. Well, that's the plan."

"That's the plan?" exclaimed Jack.

"Aye. We don't know how the Russians make contact with their fleet of submarines. It may be just a few of the trawlers, in which case we will run with the simple plan. If you find out that they routinely change the trawlers then we will need to find a way for you to provide us with information in real time, or as quickly as possible. For now, we stick with the simple plan and hope like hell that it's enough."

"So I'm going to be given a radio at some point? Possibly?"

"If it comes to that, yeah. But like I said, we will keep things simple for the time being. The less complicated the more likely it is that I will be able to buy you a drink at the Christmas office party."

"Can I get a gun too?" Jack asked, playfully.

"Yeah, and we'll fit your shoes with surface-to-air missiles," Michael said, jovially.

There was a long pause as they continued towards Galloway Park. The very chatty Michael went quiet following their brief discussion about his mission. This gave Jack the impression that for the first time, Michael was keeping something from him.

"So Michael, or do you go by Mike?"

"I do, but only by those people who want me to put them on their backs."

"Girlfriends?"

"Not exactly. Call me Mike when we get to Galloway and I'll be happy to show you what I mean," Michael explained, with friendly menace in his voice.

"Okay, Michael. What happens if it does go wrong? What if they catch me spying, or they simply decide that I am a spy without any evidence. What will they do to me?"

Michael paused for a moment before sucking a breath of air in sharply.

"My advice, if it looks like you are about to be rumbled, find some way to end it before they catch you. If they do catch you they will take you apart piece by piece until you end up confessing to being a spy. By the time they have finished you will admit to being a six foot tall, blond woman called Sharon. Seriously, it's game over if you are caught. There will be no daring rescue. In fact, we won't even admit to your existence. Your family will be told a suitable story and as far as the world is concerned, you will be dead. One of the things that you will do later is sit down and make your will. Not much fun, but we have to plan for the worst."

"I suppose."

Another long pause.

"Michael, you have been at this for a while and you know what Reilly and his mates are really like. Do you believe that they will really carry out our wishes after we are dead?"

"As long as you haven't asked for a statue of yourself to be erected in the middle of Glasgow, I'm sure they'll do their best to respect your wishes."

"And our pay? Will it really go to our families after we die?"

"Yes," replied Michael.

"How can you be so sure? What's to stop them from doing whatever they want? Our families will never know what they are entitled to."

"We make sure that they stick to their commitments. The brass are capable of many things, but for them to cross that particular line would be suicide. Literally."

That answer was good enough for Jack.

Jack had only been to Galloway Park once before—an

adventure weekend when he was still at school. Jack and Harry got into trouble within an hour of arriving—smoking behind the girls' tents. On the second day they got into a fight with some lads from Aberdeen—Jack got a black eye and a bloody nose—Harry, as usual, walked away without a mark. The weekend took place in June and Scotland was enjoying a rare hot spell. The park in winter, under several inches of snow, was a world away from his childhood recollections. The bus from school trip had entered the park through the main entrance—Her Majesty's secret services had their very own entrance, clearly marked with a series of MOD warning signs. It occurred to Jack that had the Russians wanted to identify seasoned spies and spies in training, all they would have to do was set up somewhere in the nearby countryside armed with a camera fitted with a long lens. He almost shared his insight with Michael before catching himself on—anything that he could think of had already been thought of by men who were much more intelligent and competent than him—or so he hoped.

"It's a fairly simple exercise," Michael explained, as he and Jack stood face to face in a forest clearing. "Try to stab me."

He handed a shocked Jack a hunting knife with a thick rubber handle and a short chunky blade.

"Are you serious!" Jack said, with alarm.

"Deadly serious. And I want you to really come at me. Don't hold back."

"But that's hardly fair."

"Okay Jack," Michael said, with a sigh. He produced a second knife and offered it to Jack.

Jack looked at him with confusion. Michael smiled before holstering the knife.

"Seriously mate, there is no way that you will get to me, no matter how hard you try," Michael said, confidently.

"How can you be so sure?" Jack protested.

Michael turned around and he started to walk away from Jack.

"Because Jack, in football, in war, in every possible activity, when have the Scots ever beaten the English?"

Jack lunged forward, but not using the knife, and not in anger. He simply wanted to teach the Geordie a small lesson in humility. Michael wasn't an easy man to teach. Jack wasn't sure how it happened, only that it happened really quickly and that he took a crack to the head when he landed on his back.

"What the..." Jack groaned.

"One nil to me. England!"

Michael smiled as he offered Jack a hand and helped him to his feet. Jack rubbed the back of his head and checked his fingers for blood—there was none.

"What you did wrong there mate was to let me throw you onto your arse. It's best to avoid being thrown onto your arse in a fight. You stand a better chance of winning that way," Michael added, grinning.

With Michael still holding his hand as he helped Jack to his feet, Jack took the chance and once again lunged at Michael. Once again Michael moved gracefully, with lightning speed, and once again Jack ended up on his back in the snow. Michael grinned again.

"Two nil," Michael said. "The first thing that you are going to have to learn is how to fall on your arse without causing serious damage. You banged your head twice and each time you do that you become weaker. You will end up in a vicious cycle and your opponent will have won. Over ninety percent of fights are lost by the man who takes the first fall."

"Seriously?" Jack asked.

"No, I just made that statistic up, but the reality can't be a kick in the arse off that figure."

"So Mike, just how am I supposed to fall without causing damage, especially when I'm fighting a handy son of a bitch such as yourself?"

"Bring your knees up towards your chest, and your chest

down towards your knees. Curve your spine and tighten the muscles in your back."

Michael gave Jack a few moments to process the information before he moved without warning once again and he threw him onto his back for the third time. The fall hurt like hell but Jack's head didn't make contact with the ground. In fact, this fall made him feel more alert and ready to continue as the surge of adrenalin that was present during the first two falls was not cancelled out this time by the dizzying blow to his head. Jack didn't need to be helped to his feet and even though Michael had once again thrown him to the ground, Jack felt that he had somehow won in some small way. In fact, Jack quickly realised that when fighting someone as skilled as Michael, then loosing without sustaining permanent damage was the best he could hope for. One day he would be as expert as his new friend and colleague, but there would be many falls until that day finally arrived.

An old wooden hut was the venue for his next set of lessons. His instructor was Major Clive Kendall. Kendall was a short humourless man who spoke with such natural authority that everything he said sound believable. It was the voice of a working class officer who had soldiered hard to earn his rank and he was going to make every man under his command soldier hard too.

"Our assessment of your security situation suggests that it will be safe for you to bring a camera with you," Kendall explained. "In fact, you are going to bring two cameras with you. One to photograph those trawlers that you suspect are involved in the re-supply operation, and one to take touristy kind of photographs with. This will be your decoy camera and we want you to leave it sitting around in your room, and that kind of thing. You know? Make them think that you have nothing to hide."

"I have never shown any interest in photography before," Jack explained. "They might be a wee bit suspicious if I suddenly turn into Lord Lichfield."

"It was a Christmas gift from your family. They want you to send back some photographs of the places that you visit and the wildlife. It doesn't really matter what story you use, just keep it simple and believable. They are going to be suspicious of you no matter what you do."

Jack wanted to argue with Kendall but he knew that his mind had been made up on the matter. If the camera looked as if it was going to cause him trouble then it could always meet with an unfortunate accident, or it could get stolen.

As Michael had done before him, Kendall went on to explain what was expected of Jack on his first mission. He was to take things slowly to begin with. What he learned would be held back until he returned to the UK. The second mission would be a bit more active. He would make contact with a handler when he was on shore leave and pass along intelligence to that individual. Ominously, Kendall made no mention of any missions beyond the second one.

"What happens if they capture me and force me to talk?" Jack asked.

"To be honest, if they torture you there won't be a lot that you can do other than talk. I will provide you with a file of bogus secrets that you can feed to them over the course of the interrogation. I would advise you to learn that information well. If you are captured there will not be a rescue attempt. A military incursion into Russia would precipitate a conflict. A conflict that we simply can't win. Do not give up all hope if you are captured. From time to time we arrange prisoner exchanges with the Russians. You never know, you might be lucky."

There was something about how Kendall said this last statement that gave Jack the distinct impression that it was untrue. He didn't believe for one moment that the Russians would ever give up a captured spy to secure the freedom of one of their own men. And to be honest, it didn't sound like something their side would do either. Even if there was such an exchange, Jack felt certain that there were more valuable members of the spy community currently languishing in Soviet jails who the service would rather have back.

"If you believe that you have been compromised and that your life, or your freedom, is in danger, you are authorised to kill, and you should do everything in your power to make it to friendly shores. It is unlikely that the Russians will risk sending in a team after you. If they launched an armed mission into Canada they would bring the Americans into any ensuing conflict."

"They would really go to war over something as simple as that?" Jack asked.

"Probably not, but the Americans could use it as a pretext for detaining the entire Russian fishing fleet. If that happens, who knows where it might end. Our trans-Atlantic cousins don't always think things through."

Jack sat back in his seat and he sighed. It suddenly hit him—one simple mistake on his part and the world could end up going to war. It was a sobering thought.

Back in the clearing Michael was waiting for him to begin the second round of combat training. There were over a dozen knives of varying shapes and sizes lying on a small plastic sheet on the ground. Next to the knives was another plastic sheet that was covered with various household items—an electrical lamp, a spanner and the leg of a table, to name a few.

"I hope you don't mind, but I thought we could kill two birds with one stone," Michael explained.

"Huh?" Jack said.

"Your second combat training session and the session on turning everyday objects into weapons. I thought we would get both out of the way in one go."

"OK," Jack said, as if he had any say in the matter.

The session went well. He learned how to use a knife to immobilise, silence and even kill a man. The use of the household objects as weapons was pretty much what he had been expecting. The cord of the lamp for strangulation, the spanner to club a man to death and so on. Where to strike a victim to cause varying degrees of damage was useful information to have and by the time he had finished the training exercise he had a good idea how to knock a man to the ground so that he remained conscious, but unable to fight; how to hit him in such a way as to leave him unconscious, and how to hit him in such a way that he never gets up again.

When the session had finished they went back to the hut for some lunch. That is when Michael dropped a particularly unpleasant bombshell. The three men had just sat down to some hot vegetable broth and bread.

"Later I will show you how to build a shelter," Michael explained. "There isn't a hell of a lot of snow about, but I know a few places where it is deep enough for what we need to do."

"A shelter in the snow?" Jack replied. "Doesn't exactly sound warm."

"The Eskimos seem to manage," Kendall said, with mild annoyance.

"That's all very well for the Eskimos," Jack protested. "But in case you haven't noticed, I'm not a bloody Eskimo."

"It's not exactly five star accommodation, but if you do have to escape into the frozen Russian winter then this could come in very useful," said Michael. "Besides, after a night in the shelter you will see for yourself just how cosy it can be."

Jack smiled. Michael and Kendall did not smile. When it dawned on Jack that Michael was serious the smile quickly dropped from his face.

"You have to be kidding me," Jack protested.

Michael shook his head and smiled, before continuing.

"Believe me Jack, you need to do this. If you find yourself out in the cold you will have very little time to get your shelter built before exposure kills you. I have stayed in shelters like the one that you are going to build, many times. You will be surprised just how comfortable it is."

"As comfortable as my hotel room?" Jack asked.

"Much better than your hotel room," Michael added. "There is no shower or television, mind."

The more he thought about it the colder he felt. After lunch Michael took Jack out into the woods for a spot of target practice. Jack had only fired a gun once. It was his uncle's single barrell shotgun and the kick from the antique weapon had left his shoulder sore and bruised. None of the weapons used by Michael were the size of a shotgun, but that didn't help alleviate the growing sense of dread that had settled in his stomach as Michael ran through the safety check.

"In spite of what you might have seen on television or in films, when you have a gun in your hands you will keep it pointed at the ground most of the time. In the event of an accidental discharge you are less likely to injure or kill some innocent bystander that way. Keeping your gun pointed down also makes it more difficult for someone to take the weapon from you. When you enter a room and you are not certain who is in there, having the weapon aimed at this angle gives you two important options."

Michael demonstrated by pointing the handgun he was holding at an angle in front of him.

"If you do encounter a threat then you can fire and hit them in the legs or in the stomach. This will give you time to take a second shot to finish him off. If there are only innocent bystanders in the room and the gun accidentally goes off, then you will not have killed anyone. Understood?"

Jack nodded his head, yes. Michael continued.

"Before we talk about techniques, the best thing that you can do at this stage is to have a go with some of the guns."

He handed Jack the pistol he was holding.

"Now Jack. Nothing too fancy. Just aim for one of the nearby trees and squeeze the trigger gently."

Jack's hand began to tremble a little as he took aim at a large Scots pine about thirty years away. The crack from the gun echoed through the forest and the muzzle kicked upwards. Several small pieces of bark exploded from the trunk of the tree. Before Michael had a chance to say another word, Jack fired again. Then again and again until the clip was empty.

Michael grinned at him.

"Not bad Jack. There isn't a tree in Scotland that doesn't feel scared right now. The Smith and Wesson .45 is a handy wee tool. It is powerful enough to take down most targets, but unless your first shot is incredibly lucky, you will need a second or third shot to finish the job. Now for something a little more exciting. I have placed a few targets in the snow out there in the trees. All you have to do is hit them. My wife would be extremely grateful if you didn't shoot me when you are at it. At least I hope she would."

Michael showed Jack how to change the clip in the weapon and then he sent him into the trees. Jack walked through the trees for almost five minutes before turning to Michael for help. When he turned around, Michael had vanished. Try as he might he simply couldn't see any targets. Just as he was about to return to his starting position he heard movement behind him. He turned around to see a man shaped target rising up out of the snow. Jack hesitated for a moment, and then he fired, hitting the target first time.

"Good shot Jack," an unseen Michael called. "But I think he got you first. Point and shoot. Ask questions later."

Jack looked around but he could not see Michael. There was more movement off to his left. Jack pointed the gun and fired as the target was rising up out of the snow. He didn't have time to congratulate himself before another target rose up from the snow. He hit that target too. He was excited. Adrenalin raced through his body and heightened his senses. Another target. Bang. Another. Bang. He spun round one last time to meet another target. This one sounded a little different. Aim, fire. There was a high-pitched ringing sound inside Jack's head when he realised what he had done. He raced towards Michael as he lay on the snow. Michael was completely motionless.

6

Out in the Cold

Jack dropped to his knees in the snow beside Michael. He didn't know where to start. Michael's eyes were closed and his face was pale, but to Jack's great relief there was signs of breathing as clouds of condensation formed around Michael's lips. Jack searched Michael's body for the point where the bullet entered. With a bit of luck the major organs and arteries would be untouched. Jack shifted the thick coat Michael was wearing extremely cautiously—if the bullet was lodged close to a vital organ then even the slightest movement could prove fatal. He could not find the entry point. He examined Michael's head, but again there was nothing. Jack was just about to run back in the direction of the hut in search of help when Michael suddenly moved. He grabbed Jack by the arm and stuck a pistol in his face.

"Bang, you're dead mate," Michael said.

A huge grin spread across Michael's face.

"But, I shot you. Were you wearing a bulletproof vest?"

"No mate. The last round was a blank. Just a wee joke that I like to play on new recruits."

"For god's sake, you almost gave me a heart attack. I really thought I had killed you. It's a bloody stupid thing to do. What if you had miscounted?"

"When your life is at stake, you learn to get your sums right."

Michael got up.

"Let's see your weapon," Michael said.

Jack handed him the gun. Michael looked carefully at the gun.

"I knew the number of targets and the number of live rounds before you came to the blank. I was as safe as houses."

He pointed the gun at Jack's chest and squeezed the trigger. Jack jumped when the gun went off.

"You bloody idiot," Jack yelled. "That was the blank!"

Michael's face drained of blood and a look of genuine shock set in. He held that pose for a few moments before the grin returned, even bigger than before.

"God Jack, you really are easy," Michael mocked, in a friendly way. "Two blanks, my old mucker."

"You arsehole. You complete and utter arsehole," Jack said, before storming off.

It took Jack a little while to get over the excitement of the afternoon, but once the initial sting that he had felt by being made fun of subsided, he did see the funny side of what had happened. It was just the kind of thing he would have done had he been in Michael's position.

At just after three, as the sunlight was beginning to weaken and the daytime gave over control of the skies to the night time, Jack and Michael headed off along a poorly maintained track on a steep incline. Michael had handed Jack a heavy rucksack back at the hut. The provisions it contained would sustain him until morning, or beyond, if his two instructors felt so inclined. The rucksack was heavy but it wasn't anything that Jack's strong shoulders couldn't carry.

After over half an hour trekking along the track, they came to a halt at the bottom of a small, exposed rock face. At the base of the rock face a ten foot high pile of snow had collected. Michael opened his rucksack and produced a tiny shovel.

"It goes without saying that should you find yourself in this situation for real, you probably won't have a shovel. You will have to use what you find lying around—a flat piece of stone, or a bit of wood," Michael said, before getting stuck into the pile of snow with the shovel. He dropped to his knees as he furiously pulled snow out of the pile, and then lobbed it behind him. After about ten minutes he had managed to carve a fairly sizable hole in the snow — it was big enough to hold two men with ease. Jack wondered if Michael intended to sleep out overnight with him.

Michael went into the snow cave head first. He turned once he was inside and then he poked his head out through the opening.

"Have a wee look," Michael said.

Jack got down on his knees at the entrance to the shelter and he peered inside.

"The bigger you can make it without it collapsing, the better," Michael explained. "The next step in the process is to insulate the inside of the walls. Pack as many small branches and grass in here as you can manage. It is important that you make yourself a mattress to keep your clothing off the snow. Some of the snow will melt because of the heat from your body and the last thing you want is for your clothes to get wet. If that happens then the game really will be over."

Michael climbed back out of the hole and he stood up.

"The snow that you excavate needs to be spread out. If you leave it in a pile then you will give your position away. When you are lining the inside of the shelter start by putting thick branches next to the snow to build a frame, then thinner branches, then twigs or if there is any — dry grass. Essentially, you want to make yourself a wee nest."

Jack smiled, though wee nest or not, he still wasn't looking forward to spending the night in a hole in the snow.

"Now Jack, you only have about an hour before the light gets too poor to see. It gives snow later so you can expect it to be a dark night, but at least it should be a little warmer than it has been of late. Shouldn't be any colder than minus 3 or minus 4. Make sure that you leave enough branches and grass at the entrance to the shelter so that you can plug the hole once you are inside."

Jack looked around the forest for material to line the shelter. There wasn't a lot of readymade insulating material on offer. He had to cut some fresh branches off a few of the trees. He walked into the woods. He turned to ask Michael if he had brought an axe. Michael was gone. This was it, he thought. From that point forward he was on his own. He walked towards the shelter where he had left his rucksack. When he was about ten yards from the shelter he was hit in the face by a strong, warm wind, which knocked him onto his back. Lumps of frozen snow landed on the ground all around him, and a few small pieces hit his face, stinging his skin.

He looked up in time to see a small cloud of smoke rising into the air above where the shelter had once been.

"You crazy bastard," Jack mumbled, under his breath.

It took him over ten minutes to dig the rucksack out from under the snow that had been blasted on top of it during Michael's demolition job of the shelter. He opened it. There was a box of matches, two chocolate bars, a dry jumper and trousers and a lot of big rocks. Jack swore again under his breath. Had it not been for the fact that he wasn't entirely sure where Michael was, and that he wasn't entirely confident that Michael wouldn't kill him, he would have turned and headed back to the hut. He sat in the snow for a few minutes as he planned what to do next. He got up and started searching for the tools that he needed to get the job done. He tried several pieces of slate before he found one that felt comfortable to dig with. The stone was nowhere as efficient as the shovel, but after a while Jack managed to make a hole in the snow large enough for him to squeeze into.

He climbed inside and made it larger by shaving snow from the walls. Next came the lining and insulation. It took him some time to break enough branches and to drag them back to line the shelter, but he eventually made it. Rushes and dry grass stuffed between the braches afforded him the protection that he needed to survive the cold night air. He pulled the dry clothes from the rucksack over the top of the clothes he was already wearing. He slipped into the shelter and then closed the entrance with more branches, twigs and grass. From the inside he jammed the rucksack, less the stones, up against the material in the entrance—he could not feel a draft coming through the opening. He left the pile of snow that he had dug out of the shelter where it fell—there simply wasn't enough time to scatter it properly as Michael had instructed.

As he relaxed into the relative warmth and security of his handiwork, Jack felt proud of what he had accomplished. The feelings of pride soon gave way to boredom and apprehension as the night closed in. The wind blowing through the trees sounded like the ocean—but it was an angry, unsettling sea. The sounds from the night creatures as they went about their business brought him out of semi consciousness more than once. All in all it was a restless night. He wasn't quite sure when it happened, and even less sure about how it happened, but sometime during the very early hours of the morning, he finally fell asleep—exhaustion finally getting the better of him. The sleep didn't last long. Sunlight flooded into the shelter as Michael pulled the packing material out of the entrance.

"Bloody hell mate," Michael began. "Are you going to sleep all day?"

Michael extended a hand for Jack to take. Soon they were on their way back to the hut. The previous evening Jack had been angry with Michael—the explosion, the stones in the rucksack and the lack of provisions. He had spent most of the night planning what he was going to say to him in the morning. As they walked back to their base all of those well rehearsed rebukes faded away. He had survived the night, in spite of Michael's efforts, and perhaps that was the best rebuke he could give him? He set in his mind not to let Michael see how annoyed the events of the previous evening had left him. If they wanted someone who would remain cool under pressure, then he would be an ice man.

Kendall was grinning sadistically when Michael and Jack walked into the hut.

"Good night?" Kendall asked.

Jack nodded and then said, "Yeah, not bad. A bit long and boring, but it wasn't cold or uncomfortable. In fact, I can't remember when I last had such a restful night's sleep."

Jack's words hit Kendall hard and the grin vanished.

"So guys, what's on the menu for today then?" Jack asked, with a cheeriness that verged on the sarcastic—it was subtle enough to slip past his comrades but it would have been spotted right away by one of his friends or a member of his family.

"That Jack," Michael began, "is it. All that remains for us to do is to give you your equipment and take you back to Glasgow. From there you will slip back into your normal daily routine and in a week you will head back to work. Oh, I almost forgot about your will. We can jot a few things down before we leave. Or you can sign a blank piece of paper and let me write it for you? That's it mate. We are done."

"Really?" Jack began. "One day of training and I am a fully qualified spy. God, it's no wonder that the Russians are winning the intelligence war."

"You are hardly a fully qualified spy just yet," Michael said. "You are qualified to carry out the task that you have been set. That's all. If and when the time comes for the terms of your engagement to be modified, you will receive further training. That's when I really get the chance to have some fun with you."

Michael smiled. Jack smiled back.

Kendall set a cardboard box down on the table.

"This is your equipment. In addition to the two cameras and several rolls of film, we have also included a pair of binoculars. You want to have a look at the wildlife during your next stint at sea," Kendall explained.

Jack didn't like the fact that they had once again altered the conditions of his mission, and it gave the impression that they had not thought it through. He said nothing. Writing his will took less than five minutes—the process left him feeling a little depressed—had he really achieved so little?

During the drive back to Glasgow Michael was every bit as friendly and forthcoming as he had been on the drive down to Galloway Forest Park. He told Jack how he thought that all new recruits should have at least a couple of months training, but he also reassured him by saying that the training that he had just received was going to be more than adequate for his mission. He talked a little about some of the more advanced training courses that he could look forward to in the future, such as how to survive interrogation, and how to escape from prison. The course on improvised explosive devices was a favourite of his—he even taught the CIA some of his techniques—the CIA later went on to teach those same methods to insurgents fighting in Soviet occupied Afghanistan.

Michael suggested that Jack should make a point of learning how to speak Spanish as the missions in South America were little more than extended holidays. Although Jack had picked up quite a bit of Russian during his time at sea, there were still many conversations where he was left feeling dazed and confused. If he was going to learn any new language then it would be Russian.

"It makes sense," Michael began. "It would certainly come in handy during your current mission. During interrogations the Russians have been known to revert to regional dialects to throw the foreigner being interrogated off balance. They can be very funny about their language. Most places you visit around the world the locals see it as a courtesy when someone tries to learn their language. Not so with the Russians. I guarantee that if you went back to your ship and started to speak in fluent Russian you would be sitting down in front of a couple of nice men from the KGB within hours. The Chinese are almost as bad. Learn it, just don't let them know."

Jack listened politely to what Michael had to say but that didn't mean that he necessarily agreed with everything. Jack believed that his men would have appreciated it if he knew how to speak their language fluently. It would certainly make taking the piss out of them more enjoyable.

They pulled up in front of the hotel in the Land Rover.

"A couple of wee things before you go," Michael began. "It is not enough that you say you have the binoculars and camera to look at wildlife, and to photograph it. You have to get out there and do it. Show the crew your new toys and let them have a look at them. Let them examine them and if they ask, let them borrow them. They have to believe that you are for real. And do you know what Jack, they will never buy it. No matter how good you are. So I give you this one last piece of advice, and it is the most important thing that I have told you over the last 24 hours. Do not take any risks. If you go back to the boat and there is a new crewmember who takes an interest in you, dump the second camera in the ocean. If they keep asking about the binoculars, give them away to one of the crew as a gift—say you are bored with the wildlife, or something. There are two ways for a mission to fail. One, you return without any intelligence. And two, you don't return at all. Good luck Jack, and I'll see you in a couple of months."

Michael extended a hand for Jack to take, which he did. Jack got out of the Land Rover and just as he was about to close the door, Michael added, "If you do have to take a shot at someone, make sure that the bullets aren't blanks. If you don't check the bastard might get back up and make up sleep in a hole in the snow."

Michael smiled widely and Jack returned with a wide, sincere smile of his own. He closed the door and waved as Michael drove off. The street at the front of the hotel was busy. Jack took a few moments to look at the people on the footpath and in their cars as they drove past. He smiled to himself. To all the world he looked like an ordinary man—a little dirtier and a lot less rested than most ordinary men, but he was an ordinary man nevertheless. If only they knew of the risks that he was about to take in order that they might have a future. Pride filled his chest as he walked up the steps into the hotel. He was tired but felt alive. A hot bath and a good night's rest and he would feel like a new man.

So caught up was he by the feeling of joy in that moment that he didn't notice the woman standing on the footpath on the opposite side of the street. She had been waiting for his return. The woman made a mental note of when he returned and who he was with before walking away.

The following week Jack found it hard to slip back into his normal routine. He spent as much time as he could with his family, including the noisy nephews and nieces. It had been a long time since he last sat down with his mother for a long talk—the last time had been just after his father died. He made a point of spending several hours just talking to her, about her life, about his father, about her family and how her life used to be in the old days. If he didn't come back from one of his missions he wanted her to have that quality time to look back on and draw strength from. It was a small gift but Jack believed it would mean more to her than money from the Ministry of Defence.

In that week Jack got closer to his entire family than he had been in a long time. So much so that he was genuinely sad to say goodbye. He carefully packed his equipment into a thick duffle bag and he resolved never to let the bag out of his sight. He took in as much of the city as he possibly could on the taxi ride to the airport. As the plane hurtled down the runway and lifted off he wondered if he would ever see his homeland again.

7

Unnatural Selection

After a week back onboard the ship Jack still hadn't plucked up the courage to take a camera or the binoculars beyond his quarters. There was more light in the evenings and the weather had warmed up considerably—it was just below freezing, but it remained fairly overcast with frequent snow, sleet and rain. There simply wasn't anything worth looking at. He had a small safe in his room. He kept the decoy camera, the binoculars and his wallet in the safe. This was sure to be opened and inspected by his Russian employers and he wondered how long it would be before he had to answer questions. The camera that he was going to use to photograph the trawlers was hidden in a hole that he cut into his mattress. If the camera was discovered then he really would be in trouble—he hoped that they were not as competent as Michael said they were.

On the Tuesday of his second week back on board the ship he was finally presented with the opportunity that he had been so patiently waiting for. It was a glorious day. There wasn't a cloud in the sky and the sea was unseasonably calm. Jack was having a walk on the top deck following an early morning shift in the engine room when two of the Russian crewmen started to point at something out in the water. They were excited, as far as any Russian ever got excited, and Jack joined them to have a look for himself.

A pod of blue whales was playing in the water about four hundred yards from their vessel. Jack counted at least four of the animals. The creatures weren't an unusual sight in that area but it was unusual to see them acting quite so playfully at that time of the year. From what little of the conversation that the Russians were having that he understood, the men viewed the whales' behaviour as a good omen.

Jack watched the animals for a few minutes. Then it hit him. He smiled at the Russians and then he hurried off the deck and back to his room. He returned with his camera and binoculars a few minutes later. He offered the binoculars to one of the Russians who took the binoculars off Jack without hesitation. Jack began to take photographs of the animals. The presence of the camera didn't raise so much as an eyebrow. The animals remained in view for half an hour, and before they disappeared for good almost half the crew had been up to the deck to look at them. His binoculars were used by many of his crewmates, much to Jack's delight. Half the crew now knew that he had a camera. He was out. He had taken the first big step and if things went according to plan his camera would become such a common sight onboard the ship that no one would look twice when he took it out.

Jack made a very detailed mental note of where everything was in his room over the next few days, before he left to go on a shift. As far as he could tell on his return, nothing had been moved. They either didn't view him and his camera as a threat or they were trying to lull him into a false sense of security in the hope that he would make a mistake. In an odd way he had hoped that his camera would be scrutinised — after all, it contained nothing but innocent pictures. That might put him completely beyond suspicion. Nothing happened.

It was Robert's birthday. Jack and the other two members of his team had bought him a bottle of vodka. They sat in the engine room as they quickly lowered the entire bottle. It was irresponsible for such an important team to all get drunk at the same time, but out on the high seas, onboard a Russian ship, there were very few rules. As long as the engines were running smoothly, no one cared what they got up to. The Russians were singing songs and telling jokes—both activities made Jack feel a little left out. Another bottle of vodka appeared from somewhere and the celebrations stepped up a gear. At one point during the merriment Rostislav and Ruslan stood behind Robert and they put their arms around his shoulders.

"Jack, you take photo," Ruslan ordered.

Like a good sailor, Jack obeyed. He took the camera out of its case and he set up the shot. The mood in the room suddenly turned very dark. Robert jumped to his feet and he turned away from Jack.

"No photo!" he snapped.

Rostislav, Ruslan and Jack looked at one another. It had been a very passionate and unexpected reaction. Jack tried to lighten the mood.

"Come on mate. Just a wee photo. The camera won't steal your soul, I promise."

He raised the camera again.

"No photo!" yelled Robert. He looked really uncomfortable. More than that, he looked really frightened.

It was pretty clear to Jack that Robert was never going to allow the photograph to be taken.

"It's probably for the best," Jack said, in a calm voice. "An ugly git like you would probably break the camera."

They returned to the drinking and singing but the mood had most definitely changed. Everything now seemed so forced and insincere and Jack was relieved to finally escape the underlying tension that had entered the engine room. His relief was short lived. Why had Robert acted in such an unusual way? No matter how many seemingly credible explanations he came up with he couldn't help but be drawn back to the most obvious and most frightening one—Robert was a KGB officer. The conclusion left Jack feeling nervous as he replayed in his mind the many conversations that he had with Robert over the last number of years. He had made many disparaging comments about Russians and the Soviet way of life, but these had been made in jest—would Robert have picked up on his sense of humour, or did he consider earnestly everything Jack had said?

The following morning Jack went down to the engine room a little earlier than usual. Robert was due to be on duty with him and Jack hoped to have a word with him before they started their shift, to gauge his mood and try to catch some insight into what he was thinking. Rostislav and Ruslan were sitting by the main engine looking very sorry for themselves.

"Did you have a good night?" Jack asked, trying to sound as cheerful and normal as possible.

The men just groaned at him. Jack busied himself with his normal engine room routine. He checked the fuel levels; the pressure on the boilers; the power output from the generators—everything was as it should be in spite of the lack of attention the equipment had received during the night. Robert was late for his shift. After he was ten minutes late Jack turned to the two men.

"Could one of you go to Robert's quarters and give him a shout?"

Rostislav and Ruslan both shook their heads. Jack put on his serious face and voice. He was not in the mood for their Russian intransigence.

"Now guys. You can't leave until Robert arrives, so the sooner you get off your arses and get him, the sooner you can go to bed."

The men groaned again.

"He is gone," Rostislav said, in a dead monotone.

"What do you mean, he is gone? Gone where?"

The men shrugged their shoulders.

"He can't just have gone. That doesn't make any sense. Was he ill?"

They shrugged their shoulders again.

"When did he leave? On what boat?"

"He gone ten minutes," Ruslan said, slurring his words. "Captain Ulyana's ship."

Rostislav angrily rebuked Ruslan in Russian. He spoke too quickly for Jack to make out the full rebuke, but he did pick out the words "shot" and "also".

Jack had no idea what was going on and it left him feeling really vulnerable. He tried to come up with an excuse to leave the engine room. Nothing sounded plausible. In the end he opted for something that they would respond well to—the direct approach.

"If the Captain wants to get rid of one of my team than he damn well better have someone lined up to replace him," Jack said.

Jack stormed out of the engine room. He hurried down the corridor, checking behind him as he went. He turned off for his quarters rather than for the bridge, again checking to make certain that no one was behind him. He opened the safe and removed the binoculars which he went on to hide in his coat. Trying to remain calm he quickly made his way up to the top deck. In the distance he could see Captain Ulyana's trawler steaming away from them. The view through the binoculars was crystal clear. He could see two sailors standing on deck and one of them was smoking. Everything looked normal. Within a few minutes one of the doors to the deck opened and Robert, two sailors and Captain Ulyana stepped out. Robert turned to face the Captain. He was waving his arms around frantically. He was certainly excited about something, Jack thought.

Without warning, and in a single, terrifying moment, Captain Ulyana produced a gun and she shot Robert in the head. Jack breathed in sharply as Robert's dead body hit the deck. The Captain waved her arms and two of the men dragged Robert's lifeless body across the deck. They attached something to his legs and then they rolled his corpse off the deck into the water. The body vanished almost instantly beneath the waves. Jack couldn't help himself—he moved forwards. His movement induced a response on the other ship as they all turned to face him. One of the sailors on her ship handed Ulyana a pair of binoculars. It was only when she was looking right at him that it occurred to Jack to move. He quickly slipped in behind some of the rigging. He crept along the length of the ship until he found a small gap between two shipping crates. He positioned himself so that he could take another look at the other boat without being spotted. His blood turned cold. He watched as the other vessel completed the manoeuvre. They were heading back towards him.

8

Search and Rescue

Jack stayed as close to the deck as he could as he scampered towards the nearest door. He slipped back into the bowels of the vessel. The frantic journey through the metal corridors went without incident, and soon he was back in the engine room. He ignored his workmate as he paced the dirty floor in a search for a way out. Try as he might he couldn't think of a safe way off the ship. He took a seat on a wooden crate in the corner of the room that was as far away from the entrance to the room as he could manage. He cursed himself many times over in those few desperate minutes before the Captain entered the room. He cursed himself for being so arrogant as to believe that he could handle himself in this world. He cursed himself for not insisting that an escape option be put in place. He cursed himself for the pain and suffering that his death or "disappearance", would cause to his family. But most of all, he cursed himself that he had no substantial weapon at hand that he could use to go down fighting.

The door swung open and two giant Russians entered the room ahead of the Captain. The Captain barked an order in Russian and the two men began to search the engine room. It was a pretty rough search as the men overturned crates and emptied toolboxes. Their intention was not to find anything but to let Jack and his workmate know that they meant business. This was the Captain's subtle way to let them know that if they were to admit to their sins before their sins were uncovered then she might make what followed a little bit easier on them. Neither Jack nor his workmate had any intention of giving her what she wanted. Jack remained seated and he tried his best not to look concerned — whatever was going on was none of his business and he was happy to sit quietly and keep his nose out of it. The Captain had other ideas.

Slowly and with the purpose of intimidation, she walked across the room and stood in front of Jack.

"Jack," she began. "It would seem that we had a spy in our midst. His intention was to sabotage the fleet and kill as many of us as he possible could. You included."

Jack looked stunned. Who was Robert? Was he one of ours? Was he working for the Americans? Regardless of who he was working for, why had no one thought it worth their while to let him know that there was another spy working with him? Maybe it was just as well that he didn't know.

"Really?" Jack said, with mild surprise. "He seemed like such a normal guy. Sure, he was a bit... Well, a bit, Russian."

The Captain smiled.

"Aw Jack. You have such a way with words," she said. "A lesser man would be worried with all this going on, but not my Jack. That famous British backbone that I hear so much about."

"Scottish backbone, if you don't mind. I'd hate to be lumped together with those snivelling English."

She laughed. It was loud and hearty.

"Well Jack, it looks like my men are finishing up. Please accept my apologies for the mess we have generated, but with the safety of the entire fleet in the balance, I'm certain that you understand?"

"Of course Captain. I would have done the very same thing had I been in your shoes."

The Captain began to walk towards the door to the engine room. Jack plucked up the courage to ask her one last question before she left.

71

"Captain," he began. "Who exactly was he spying for?"

"You see Jack, my country presents a side to the world that is of complete unity and social bliss, but the reality is somewhat different. Some of the measures taken by our leaders in the past have been extreme, if necessary, and they have led to resentment building in the hearts of some men. The way that collaborators during the Nazi occupation were dispatched is just one such wellspring of dispute. When Stalin had ordered them executed he had wanted their entire families wiped out at the same time, but some of his closest advisors counselled against it. What you witnessed from the deck of this ship earlier forms part of that legacy of indecision. The great man made very few mistakes, but not irradiating that cancer when the war ended is one mistake that we are still living with. Instead of time healing that wound, time has made it grow worse. Once there were only wives and children that needed removed, but now there are grandchildren and great grandchildren all walking around with thoughts of revenge in their heads. Your former friend was one such individual."

"And your government expects humble Captain's such as yourself to clear up that mess?" Jack asked.

"My government expects any citizen from any walk of life to help in the clean-up whenever they are asked to help. That is why our country is the greatest superpower the world has even seen. That is why our empire will live on long after the empires of Britain, France and America are no more than distant memories."

"That is a nice system that you have got there. The politicians back home would give anything to carry that kind of clout."

"Like I said, it works. It may be hard for people from the West to understand why we do the things that we do, but that is their problem, not ours."

"Well Captain, just like official British policy when it comes to these matters, I am not here to interfere in how you run your affairs. If anything, I am glad that you caught him before he had a chance to carry out whatever it was that he had planned. I am happy to go along with whatever you decide."

The Captain smiled at Jack. It was a false smile—the kind she might have adopted had she just opened an unwanted gift.

"Good boy Jack. I always said that you were one of the good ones. We really must have dinner sometime. I really enjoyed our last meal together."

Jack smiled uneasily. Just as long as their next meal together wasn't his last meal, he thought. The Captain left the room, closely followed by her surly henchmen.

For the next few days life on the boat returned to some sort of normality. A replacement was brought in for Robert. Serge was Russian to the back teeth and it was quite obvious to Jack, even with his limited experience, that this man was part of the Russian espionage community. Everywhere Jack went Serge followed. At first it was really annoying but when Jack gave himself over to the fact that his shadow wasn't going anywhere, he started to have some fun with him. On one occasion he ran out of the engine room and down the corridor. He didn't stop until he was standing on the deck. Serge was built to stop spies and bullets, but he was not built for speed. He pushed his eighteen stone, six foot frame down the corridors and up to the deck as quickly as he could. When he finally caught up with Jack he was out of breath on the verge of a coronary infraction.

"Sorry big guy," Jack said. "I thought I heard a whale."

The look that spread across Serge's face was one of complete anger. Jack knew that he had gone a wee bit too far. If he did it again there was every possibility that Serge would kill him in his sleep, if only to avoid having to go for another run.

Days moved into weeks and even Serge began to lighten up. Try as they might his Russian paymasters simply could not put a finger on Jack. He had a second meal with the good Captain, but mercifully she was called away on ship's business halfway through the meal. Jack wondered which poor son of a bitch she was called away to dispatch on that occasion.

The sea had been rough all day. Heavy rain fell on the metal deck like a suspenseful drum roll. It all left Jack with a foreboding feeling in his stomach. Serge had returned to his former, surly self and the rest of the crew were being even more standoffish than usual. When he went to bed that night Jack took forever to fall asleep. He was awakened in the early hours of the morning by violently being pulled from the bed and thrown onto the floor. The light came on and an angry looking Serge was standing over him. This was the moment that he had been fearing for weeks. As Serge reached down and lifted him onto his feet Jack desperately searched his mind for the reason why it was happening now. What had they discovered? What did they suspect? Was his execution going to be the result of nothing more than the suspicions of the good Captain? A gut instinct that was warped towards a guilty verdict.

His mind was pulled back to the serious immediacy of his situation when Serge head-butted him. Jack fell back onto the floor. His head struck the metal frame of the bed on the way down. He looked up at Serge. The giant had had his fun. It was now time to end it. Serge pulled a revolver that he had tucked in the back of his trousers, and he pointed it at Jack. There was no emotion on his face as his firing finger tightened around the trigger. Jack looked away and he closed his eyes. Jack jumped when the gun went off. There was no pain. Was this what it felt like to die? He opened his eyes just as Serge fell to the ground. Standing there in the doorway was one of the bridge crew. Jack didn't really know the man. He was the second officer, or something.

"Come with me Jack. You don't have much time."

Jack paused for a moment.

"Get up now if you want to live!" the man snapped, holding out a hand.

Jack had no idea what in the hell was going on but he was certain of one thing—staying in that room waiting for Serge's replacement would be suicide. As they hurried down the corridor towards the bow of the ship Jack wondered why none of the Russian crew had come out of their quarters when the gun had gone off. Were they really so hardened to that kind of thing that the sound of gunfire didn't cause them a second thought? Maybe Serge had been to every room in the ship and Jack was merely last on his list?

The narrow staircase at the end of the corridor was wet and slippery. Jack hadn't had time to put on his boots—he did manage to snatch them off the floor as he was leaving. Once outside the full force of the storm from earlier that day was still battering their vessel. They hurried across to the wooden lifeboats at the side. The winch looked as if it hadn't been used in decades, and worse than that, it looked as if it never could be used. Jack looked for the start button as the Russian swung the hoist around the side of the ship. The lifeboat was ready to be lowered into the ocean. Jack put on his boots as he continued to study the controls.

"Here, use this," said the Russian. The man threw Jack a knife.

The man was standing on the edge of the boat with another knife, furiously cutting through one of the ropes holding the lifeboat up. Jack climbed up onto the side of the ship and he began to work on the other rope. The back end of the lifeboat swung towards Jack as the man cut through the rope. Jack calculated that one more big push on his part and his rope too would be severed. He waited for the lifeboat to enter an upward swing away from him and then he cut the rope. Both men watched intently as the boat hit the water. They watched even more intently as they viewed the boat for any signs that it had been damaged. It seemed to be fine.

"Jack, jump," the man ordered.

"But.."

"Get into the water and into the boat, or stay here and die. Those are your choices."

Jack looked down at the angry water. The lifeboat was starting to move away from the ship. He took a deep breath and jumped. The fall took forever and he was winded when he hit the water. His lungs hurt. The pain in his lungs soon gave way to the pain caused to his body by the cold water. He swam with all his might until he reached the lifeboat. Once inside the lifeboat he looked up to where his saviour had been standing. He was gone. There were several flashes of light and a few minutes later the man came back into view. He teetered on the edge of the boat before tumbling over the railings into the water. Jack desperately scanned the water where the man's body had landed, but he was nowhere to be seen. Jack looked up on hearing the first burst of automatic gunfire. Two men were standing on the edge of the ship firing at him. The first couple of bursts were merely finding the range; the next bursts would end it. In a desperate act of self-preservation he moved to the far side of the lifeboat. He looked up just as a ball of fire exploded behind the gunmen. The force from the explosion was enough to send the men over the edge into the water. There was another explosion on the ship, quickly followed by yet another. He fixed the oars to the holders and he began to row for all his might away from the ship. A siren sounded on the ship and more explosions sent the remaining sailors spilling into the sea. Jack's mind returned to the winch—there was no way they could have launched the remaining lifeboats if the other winches were in a similar condition.

Jack felt that there was enough distance between him and the ship to take a break. He watched the burning boat as it rose and fell on the angry sea, up and down, the fire losing intensity with each cycle until finally it was gone—the ship was gone. He lowered his head. Not all the Russians on that ship were out to kill him. Most were just ordinary men out to earn a living.

As he indulged the melancholy of the thought he didn't notice the gunman as he hauled himself into the lifeboat. The gun had gone but the knife he was carrying had a large enough blade to finish what the guns had started. The man brought the knife into a raised position as he readied himself to stab Jack in the back. Fortune was on Jack's side, as at the last moment, just as the man was beginning the fatal lunge, a large wave struck the lifeboat and upset the man's equilibrium. Jack turned around as the man fell. He had lost control of the knife. Jack sprung to action and he quickly scooped up the blade. He brought into focus his training as the man went for him. The man's lifeless body fell over the side of the lifeboat into the water. Jack lay on his back with the rain beating down on his face. This was by no means over. There was a fleet of Russian vessels out there and it would not be long before they began to close in on his position like sharks sensing a drop of blood in the water.

Jack was floating aimlessly on the water for hours. In spite of the weather, or perhaps because of it, his frozen body began to shut down and he lost consciousness. The next waking thought he had was in the sickbay of a US coastguard vessel.

9

The Irish Question

The entire mission rocked his belief in what he was doing to its very foundations. Jack never truly believe in fate but he at least believed that he had made the right decision when he had said yes to that life-changing question asked of him back in Scotland. Now battered and bruised and thoroughly unconvinced that what he had just been through had made even the slightest bit of difference to the nation's security, he was very much at a low point. All the romantic notions of heroism had left his mind and as he flew back home across the vast Atlantic he played over in his mind how he would leave this new life of his behind, if that was even possible.

He sat next to an old couple from the North West of England on the plane journey back home. During the first hour of the flight they seemed friendly enough; she did all the talking and he nodded enthusiastically and uttered, yes dear, every now and again. She nattered on about the places that they had visited and the sights they had seen. Then came the complaining.

"We were on that boat for almost three hours," she began. "And it was so cold. There is still a chill in my bones. I don't think I'll ever feel warm again. Three hours and we didn't see a single whale. I was of half a mind to ask for my money back. Isn't that right, Harry?"

"Yes dear," replied her husband, with henpecked defeat in his voice.

Jack smiled wryly. "The cold was really something, alright," he replied.

The debriefing took place in a grey, anonymous looking building in London. There was a brass nameplate by the side of the heavy, black door at the front of the building, but the corrosive atmosphere of London had long since erased all meaning that it once held.

It was a short encounter in Jack's opinion, given his near death experience, but it was a meeting that ended up being momentous in its scope. He was offered vague, though enthusiastic reassurances that what he had been through did make a difference and that many lives, perhaps even the entire nation, if it ever came down to a nuclear shootout, was in a much better state because of what he had been through. Jack nodded his head and he looked across the table stoically—that was how heroes were supposed to respond as their great achievements were recounted back to them—nonchalant to the point of apathy. Jack felt a little annoyed that his spy masters were not more forthcoming with details, but he settled down when he told himself that it was probably better that he didn't know too much—if he was ever captured then there was nothing of importance that they could get out of him. On the flipside of that argument was the fact that if he had nothing genuine to offer to his captors then he would be of no use to them.

The young intelligence officer who conducted the debrief informed Jack that he was to be allowed five days leave— the news was imparted to him with the enthusiasm of a cheesy game show host—you have just won this week's star prize! Jack did not react in kind—with these people the other shoe would drop sooner or later.

Eventually Jack relented and let go of some of his suspicion as he sighed with contentment at the thought of heading back to the safety and warmth of home for a few days, but just as he was settling into the comfort of the thought the young man told him that he was to be briefed on his next mission before he went on leave—it would never do for an agent to spend time idly enjoying himself without thoughts

.ıe job hanging over him like a dark cloud. The young man continued by reiterating the creed of secrecy that Jack should adopt when he was back in the real world—this was now the third time that this speech had been fired at him. If he was intent on going back home to tell all around him what he had really been up to, then some speech, and its associated threats was in no way going to change his mind.

"There are a number of sensitive situations in play at the moment," said the officer. "Because of those situations we have noticed an increase in activity in the Soviet intelligence community. We are trying to negotiate a prisoner exchange through the Chinese and we don't want to give the Russians a reason to walk away from those negotiations. As far as the Russians are concerned, you are dead. We need for you to stay dead. We need for you to keep a low profile. Your next mission will take you to an area where Russian spies are a bit thin on the ground."

"Where's that then?" Jack asked. "The Arctic?"

The young officer smiled.

"Not exactly. And besides, the Arctic is surprisingly active. The potential for oil exploration means that every major power has agents keeping an eye on it," the officer explained, somewhat smugly.

"Christ, just how big is the intelligence community?" Jack asked.

"Worldwide, we could be talking hundreds of thousands of agents. We are everywhere. That's why you need to be extremely careful at this time. We have already made an official request to the Russian government on behalf of your family. They have said that you died when a freak wave hit your ship. No body was recovered."

Jack smiled and said, "It is amazing how many freak waves hit Russian vessels."

"Aye, and the waves only ever take out foreigners working on those ships," replied the officer.

"So," Jack continued, with his tone turning a little more serious. "Where are you sending me this time?"

"You know that I can't tell you that. Fortunately I know a man who can," said the officer, before getting up out of his seat.

"Shall we?" the officer asked.

Jack was escorted to a large conference room and presented to half a dozen very senior members of the intelligence community. In the past the men sitting across from him all headed their own divisions, or organisations and each held a very healthy, and at times not altogether unjustified suspicion of one another. Although Jack had no idea of the significance and importance of them all coming together to meet him on that day it was a message that was not lost on everyone else working in the building. Whoever this Scot was he was important. Important enough to gather all of the most powerful government employed men in the nation. What the IRA would have given to take out any one of these individuals, never mind all of them at one time, spoke volumes of the waters Jack now swam in. The spokesman for the group was Commander Jason Deeley, a man who Jack would grow to respect and trust more than any other individual in his life. Deeley had a way of cutting through the bullshit that somehow made even the unpleasant things that he had to say seem reasonable. This trait made it easy for him to get the men under his command to do what he wanted them to do even if they stood a good chance of getting killed in the process—you will probably get shot, but we have already trained your replacement.

"Jack, you don't need to be an expert to know that the war with the Republican movement in Ireland, and here on the Mainland, is going to hell. Every day there are more bombings and shooting, and in recent times we have kidnappings thrown into the mix," Deeley explained. "Every effort we have made to break through their defences and get a man into the organisation has failed. One agent after another, lost to the Provos. It really is a situation that we can no longer tolerate. We have even tried putting pressure on active IRA men to do our bidding by carrying out the odd kidnapping of our own, but each and every time we have been knocked back. Many of the men sitting across from you have concluded that it simply isn't possible. With all due respect to those men, I think they are wrong."

It was a little unsettling that Deeley could speak of the loss of the men with annoyance rather than outrage, as if he was talking about his car keys rather than real live human beings—straight talk and no nonsense was one thing, but there was such a thing as being too blunt.

Deeley was a highly intelligent man. He was a new breed of commander who still suffered at the hands of less competent men above him. The only way that he was ever going to make a difference was by proving himself. Many within the British intelligence community still believed that the Irish were intellectually inferior and that the only thing that was really needed to sort them out was a stern, straight, rod across their backs. Brute force has been effectively employed for centuries and if the politicians would only give them a free hand they would bring them to heal in no time at all. Deeley knew better. The Republican movement had grown into one of the most sophisticated and ruthless fighting machines that the world had ever known. They were embedded in every community and their word, either by agreement, or through fear, was law. Unless the plan was to carpet bomb every town on the island of Ireland then there was no way the Republicans could ever be defeated by force alone. Deeley knew that a more intelligent, long term approach was needed if this war was ever to end. This was Deeley's chance to prove that his tactics were the future. The full extent of this pressure was not revealed to Jack during the course of the conversation, but not only was Deeley's reputation about to be placed in Jack's hands, but the entire future of the war against the terrorists lay squarely at Jack's feet.

Deeley nervously twirled his pen as he waited for a response from Jack.

"How did you get the men close enough to the IRA in the first place? I mean, they must have come into contact with them in order to get caught?" Jack asked.

Two of the police officers looked a little uncomfortable as Deeley continued. None of the men sitting across the table from Jack got to such positions of power without displaying self-belief and arrogance and if a plan formulated by any one of them had failed then there was no way that they would hold themselves to blame for that failure. If only those below them were less incompetent then the war would already be won.

"Training, Jack. And mindset. It has always been procedure, from the World Wars to the Cold War, to try to make our spies fit in. No matter how well you do, a German will always spot a non-German. Same with the Russians. And it is the same with the Irish. You can dress a bull up as a cow, but sooner or later it will be milking time. Anyone seeking to join the IRA will immediately be flagged, and these people do not give anyone the benefit of the doubt."

Jack smiled. It was a well known fact that the organisation was comprised of cells and that each member of those cells was recruited at a local level—the men and women all knew each other from the time they were children, and in many instances they were all related.

The frustrating thing was that Jack knew how to get the information that they needed to win the war. Every man sitting around that table knew how they could get the information that they needed to win the war. The four captured officers were all dead, but before they died they would have been subjected to the most horrendous torture. The torture was there as a warning to others who might have thoughts of following in their footsteps, but it was also how the IRA gained intelligence on the British operation in Ireland. If they were truly serious about beating the Provos at their own game then sooner or later they would have to employ similar tactics on captured IRA men—it was ruthless, but it was targeted and effective. The political class in Britain had not yet developed the stomach for such measures, but with each fresh atrocity their hunger deepened. Arbitrary arrests, the use of force to crush civil unrest, and all the other measures that caused so much concern within the general public were never going to be enough. It would only be a matter of time before that order finally came down and Jack hoped that he wouldn't be the one who had to carry it out. It was a very dirty war and there would be much blood on the hands of many civilised men when it finally came to an end. If the torture was carried out in private before the call for blood from the public became so heightened that public acts of suffering were necessary, then something of the nation's humanity would be preserved.

There had always been a suspicion of the intelligence community amongst the politicians—if they were given too much power, sooner or later they would turn some of that power away from fighting terrorists and spies and use it on their political masters. It had happened in Russia, Africa and all across South America—God Save The Queen would still play on, but it would be muffled under the sole of a jackboot. Almost forty years after the Second World War, the lessons learned from that time were still living history to many members of both houses of Parliament. The civilised people of Germany had happily strolled into the arms of a sadistic madman, and based on a dark fiction that was so clumsily crafted and so foolish that it was laughable—would such a move in the UK with a very real terror stalking every street really be such an outrageous possibility? Jack sincerely believed the prospect to be very real. Jack concluded that the war could be won, possibly within a few years, but the cost of winning that war would be the soul of the nation.

"Jack," Deeley said, "I believe that no matter how

convincing our officers are as actors, we will never make inroads like this. What we plan is to put in place a really convincing cover story and then wait. Should it take five years before we get any response from the Provos, then so be it. We will wait for them this time, and not force the issue. Let them come to us, rather than raise suspicion by continuing to try it the other way round."

Deeley slid the file across the table to Jack. It wasn't an overly dramatic gesture, but given just how much Deeley shunned the sensational, it somehow came across as such.

Deeley knew that the contents of the file would shock Jack. He also knew that on paper the plan would come across as a little crazy. In an effort to take the sharp edge off the contents of the file Deeley continued to explain the logic behind his pitch.

"We want you to be that agent. We don't want you to learn an Irish accent or get to know the local customs as this has been our downfall in the past. We aim to give you a credible, but, and this is the essential part, a story that is not complicated," Deeley said. There was something about the tone of his voce that suggested to Jack that the danger to his friends and family might not necessarily come from the IRA, should Jack not play ball.

"When this meeting has concluded, you will be given a few hours to look over the file. I want you to study every detail of the contents before you come to a conclusion. After that time we will expect a decision, one way or the other. You handled your last assignment with the skill of a seasoned officer. God, the very fact that you made it back alive impressed the hell out of me for a start, I don't mind telling you, I lost a fiver on you getting back in one piece. But don't worry, I won't hold that against you. Open the file, read the information carefully and then give me your decision. I won't patronise you by recounting some of the atrocities that the IRA has carried out over the years in an attempt to manipulate you, nor will I try to impress on you just how important and urgent this mission is. I will leave that decision to your conscience and better judgement. It is a dangerous mission and there is absolutely no guarantee that you will be successful, but this is an operation that will go ahead and if you don't accept it, someone else will. You are clever enough and resourceful enough to live through this. I would not be as confident if one of the other potential candidates had to take your place."

Jack smiled.

"No pressure, then," Jack quipped.

"No Jack, more pressure than you will ever have experienced in your entire life. You will be under pressure twenty-four hours a day, seven days a week, possibly for years at a time."

Jack opened the file as instructed and he read the Official Secrets Act disclaimer on the inside cover. As the men who he had been sitting across from him, and who he had not been introduced to, cleared the room, Jack moved on to the next page of the report. Jack glanced up as the last of the men left. Why had they been there, he wondered. Was it simply to add an official seal of approval to the madness of the proposal?

Deeley lingered in the doorway once the others had left the room. The contents of the report really was through the looking glass stuff. A black and white photograph of a school girl looked up at him. Her hairstyle and uniform were straight out of the fifties and the warm smile that she was wearing masked an inner turmoil that would one day be used in the fight against Republican terrorists.

"That is your mother. She was a nice Catholic girl who left Belfast for London to seek her fortune. Like so many before her things did not turn out quite as she had planned. Long story short, she had a son, Martin, and you are going to take his place. The real Martin died when he was a baby. His mother was killed in a botched police raid when she was back in Belfast visiting friends. We are going to use that incident as your motivation for moving to Belfast. Over time you will let it be known why you have returned and that you want justice for your dear old Ma. Simple story with a sound basis in fact. I really do believe this is the only way that we will ever make inroads. Downside is we will only get to play this card once.

"As a Scot with IRA sympathies we hope you will appeal to the organisation as you will be able to go to places that someone with an Irish accent would never gain access to. "

"Jack, what do you think?" he asked, impatiently.

"It all sounds fine, as far as it goes, but with such a long term commitment I have to consider my family," Jack replied.

Jack was still a bit green but he was not that green. They had asked him for one simple reason, and it had bugger all to do with how well he had performed in the Atlantic—he was Scottish. An English agent with exactly the same story would never attain the kind of access that they were looking for.

"This is a serious game. It is not only your life that is on the line. Your time in the North Atlantic tells me that you can cope well out on your own, away from friends and family, but this an altogether different prospect. You could be over there for years. Hell, you could be over there for decades. I'm not suggesting that you will not be able to see your family during your time in Ireland, but you have to understand that you will not be home to see them every other month. If there is illness or a death in the family you will be expected to carry on with the mission. We will try our very best to accommodate family circumstances, but the mission always comes first. Bottom line, your life is not my priority. I will be investing a lot of time, resources and taxpayers money in this mission, in you, and if you think that there is even the slightest possibility that you might betray that investment, save us all the time, money and frustration now and walk away.

"On a much more personal level, I have staked a lot more than a fiver on you being successful. If this strategy doesn't work then we will move onto Plan B. Plan B will take this country down a road that no civilised nation should ever contemplate. Our country will never be the same again; at least not in our lifetime. I appreciate that this is a lot to place on your shoulders but that is the reality of the situation that we currently find ourselves in. Bottom line—you simply can't fail."

With those words of warning still ringing in his Jack's ears, Deeley walked out and Jack was left in the empty room with the file and his own thoughts. Two hours later and his mind was still fixed on going through with the assignment, even if the pages he had carefully studied did bring some serious questions to the fore. None of those negatives were compelling enough to take the shine off the glory he would attain should the mission be a success. He had survived the very best that the Russian state had to throw at him and he sure as hell wasn't going to fall at the hands of rebels living across the Irish sea.

There were many descriptions of murder in the report. Everything from the up close and personal throat slitting, to the impersonal remotely detonated car bomb. What these descriptions lacked was photographic evidence. Words in black and white were still only words—a photograph of a man lying by the side of a road with a bullet hole in his head, or the charred carcass of a bomb victim, would have brought the descriptions into clearer focus. Jack wondered if all photographs, except for that of Mary Quinn, had been removed on purpose. The thought annoyed him slightly—he didn't need to be shielded from anything, no matter how terrifying. His annoyance was not manifest when he spoke to Deeley on his return.

"I'm in," Jack said, simply.

Deeley smiled warmly for the first and last time over all the years that Jack knew him.

"Welcome to the project," Deeley said, as he shook Jack's hand. "And for all our sakes, I wish you the very best of luck. We will be in contact with you over the next few weeks."

Jack smiled as he recalled the first time the Service had contacted him after he first joined. He was a different man back then. Would they really send a man into the bedroom of a sleeping, trained killer? He'd certainly give them what for if they tried. The meeting broke-up. Jack's head was spinning with all kinds of scenarios as he left the building. Although preoccupied at that moment, Jack probably would not have noticed the woman sitting in the red mini at the end of the street as he walked past her had his head been completely clear. He looked right at her, and still he didn't notice her. She certainly noticed Jack—she quickly turned her head away.

There really was no place like home, and now that he had settled somewhat into his new occupation he appreciated the normality of his friends, family and the familiar haunts that he frequented. All the old troubles still plagued the city; unemployment, poverty, fights, marriage break downs, and so on, but they were somehow comforting to him—no matter how serious those problems were, they were never quite a matter of life and death—for the most part.

"Carol Jamison has been stepping out with an Italian. Her man on the rigs and all. She always was a little hussy," Jack's mother remarked.

Jack smiled and sipped at his tea as he sat across the table from her. The smell of fresh-cut flowers filled the room. She was fanatical about flowers for two reasons—they brought colour into her life and they helped to mask the smell of stale cigarette smoke that hung around the house like an ever present spirit. Jack wished that she would cut down on the fags—the thirty a day that she was on were really taking their toll—each time he came home she looked a lot older and more jaundiced, and there was a definite rattle to her breathing that worried him. He had suggested that she went to see the doctor that last time that he came home. The suggestion was not well received.

"If I had stepped out with some other guy on your Da, he would have broken my neck," she said, with genuine feeling.

The very thought of anyone daring to stand up to his mother made Jack smile even more. Someone's neck would have been broken, but he was pretty certain that it wouldn't have been her neck.

He spent his days with his family and his evenings drinking in the pub with his friends. He was never one to forget himself and talk too much when he was drunk, but he certainly wasn't going to take any chances given the importance of the information that was floating around inside his head, just looking for an escape route.

On the last official night of his leave he went out for a pint at the Hound; a dingy drinking spot that had in recent years become a favourite of students, much to the annoyance of Jack and his drinking buddies. As he left the pub, a little lighter in the head, but still sure on his feet, he was approached by a man.

"A car will pick you up at the front of the hotel at eight in the morning," said the man, before he continued on his way. Jack framed a response but as it took him a few moments to do so, he thought it best not to shout that response after the man.

A series three Land Rover Safari was waiting for him at the front of the hotel at eight the next morning, as promised. Jack felt a little melancholy as he looked in the side mirror at the city as it shrank and then melted away. He couldn't help but feel that this would be the last time he ever saw his beloved home, or if he did make it back, he would be so changed, so damaged, that he would never view the place with the same warmth again.

The intensive training he was put through over the following few weeks took into account every conceivable scenario but it lacked one key element which was of major concern to Jack—even if he decided not to voice that concern—what did he do if he needed to get out in a hurry? There was no number to call, no handler lurking in the background with access to a fleet of helicopter gun-ships. The US coastguard would not be waiting to pick his frozen body out of the water this time around. He would be completely on his own.

The thought of being captured and tortured filled him with genuine fear. When he had looked through the file back in London he had noticed a little unimportant looking something that was positioned in such a way that he suspected he was not meant to find it. At the very back of the file, suspiciously clipped to the penultimate page was a small, letter-size piece of paper. The rest of the paperwork was A4 and had he been a slow reader this final page would surely have slipped past his scrutiny. The font was tiny, and in every conceivable respect the page looked inconsequential. Jack had carefully slid the fragile piece of paper onto the desk and he strained his eyes to read what was written upon it.

The hairs on the back of his neck had stood to attention as he read on. It was a field report, written by the commanding officer of an army base situated on the border between Northern Ireland and the Irish Republic. The report outlined the details of the discovery of a body outside the Republican stronghold of Darkly. What was described was a scene of utter horror. The army was called in to assist the police with a body that had been found by a local farmer. The mutilated body had been nailed to an oak tree on the farmer's land. The method of the victim's dispatch, and the barbarity with which the body was put on display, was straight out of medieval history. The dead man was with the SAS. He had been slowly tortured to death. His intestines had been removed and wrapped around the rest of the corpse like a macabre rope. His arms, legs and head had been severed.

The limbs were nailed to the tree, next to the torso, and the head had been spiked with a six foot long branch and put out on display in front of the rest of the remains. Birds had already set about the business of devouring the body, and the man's face had been pecked beyond recognition.

It was a horrifyingly blunt warning, and to Jack it was immensely personal. To add the final insult to his demise, the soldiers attending the scene had to take shots at the remains — the terrorists had booby trapped bodies in the past and it would be 48 hours from the time that the police had been notified before the soldiers at the scene finally removed the remains from public display.

Jack had carefully placed the page back into the file, closed the cover, and then slid it across the table in an effort to put as much distance between him and the horror contained within the file as he could manage. Jack then sighed as he sat back in the chair. This was indeed something different. He knew where he stood with the Russians. Torture was not really their thing, at least not under the current regime. They asked you a question and if they didn't like the answer that you gave, they put a bullet in your head. It was quick, clean and somewhat painless. The IRA was all about making big statements. The louder and more terrifying that statement, the better. With his heart racing inside his chest Jack simply knew that he could not say no. The dismembered body of the SAS man plagued his every waking moment, both back home in Scotland, and in London as he absorbed all the information his handlers threw at him. Any one small part of that torrent of information could mean the difference between life and death one day, but it was hard for him to remain focused. He was in this game to win, and the rewards of success were immeasurable; the horror and pain of failure unthinkable.

10

Of Saints and Sinners

The area of Belfast where he was situated was at a superficial level like any other inner city area in '70's Britain. The types of low grade homes, the businesses and the people—they were all familiar to Jack but the accent took some getting used to. The hard edges to the deep Belfast tone in the part of the city where Jack found himself embedded was an affront to his ears—the unique language of the ship builders interspersed with Gallic and Ulster Scots only served to add to his confusion and frustration. It was going to take him a long time just to understand what in the hell the people around him were going on about, let alone reaching a position where he was comfortable and confident enough to make a move on the IRA.

The house that was rented for him was cold and damp and the street that it was on was dirty, bleak and depressing. Belfast got more than its fair share of rain and the weather was an obsession of the locals. For the first few days that Jack was in the area people kept their distance and he received nothing more than a friendly nod of acknowledgment, or a suspicious glare from those he passed on the streets. In this respect Jack found Belfast to be very different to most other UK cities. In Glasgow or Birmingham suspicion and discrimination came in the form of racism. In Belfast, no one would give an Indian or Jamaican a second look—they were apart from the Northern Irish conflict—there weren't too many Indian or Jamaican IRA or UVF men. Suspicion was for people who looked very much like the man or woman down the street—this is where the real danger lay—from an enemy who looked and spoke like them.

As time dragged on Jack was beginning to wonder if he would ever make contact with what had been described to him back in London as the welcoming committee. The agents who had been killed in the last four years had all made it past the welcoming committee. Each area had a group of grassroots supporters who would be sent out to vet any stranger who entered their area. These men and women were not necessarily part of the IRA, but they were gathering intelligence on behalf of the organisation. Most of that information was not used to protect the community from outsiders, but it was used to ascertain if the stranger was in the area to conduct legitimate business—if they were there on business then the organisation would send someone along to let them know what the cost of carrying out that business would be. Those protection rackets had grown into a fully fledged industry and it was even tolerated by the authorities, for the most part, much in the same way that prostitution was tolerated in some other cities. When the government offered redevelopment grants to construction firms there was a ubiquitous, non-descript cost added to every funding package—this was normally fixed at ten percent and it was colloquially known as the service charge.

The isolation that Jack felt over the first few days of the assignment changed abruptly when a gang of six men came calling late one Thursday night. The two men who knocked on the door unceremonially pushed in past him when he opened the door. The other men stood guard outside the house in case Jack had any ideas about escape. It was a very clumsy home invasion, but as they were not wearing masks or brandishing weapons, Jack decided that he was not in any immediate danger. The calm way that he accepted the intrusion was in sharp contrast to the manic nature of the invaders.

The psychology of these men was not easily divined. How

94

he should react in order to make it through such encounters in one piece had only been glossed over during his training. It was an ethereal type of question that might easily have been asked by a newly qualified teacher as they struggled to work out how to control an unruly class—there was no right answer—the best that Jack could hope for was that the men were in the mood for a chat.

The meeting was extremely tense with heavy menace keeping Jack mentally dancing all the while. It was the moment of truth. His training and the intensive learning curve he had been on in London would be assessed in that precarious moment. As Jack sat on the mottled armchair next to the fireplace with two of the men standing in the centre of the room, he slipped into character. He began to act like his life depended on it.

"I would tell you to take a seat and ask you to stop worrying but you seem to be sorted there mate," Kieran Smyth, the taller of the two men standing in front of him and the leader of the gang, said in a deliberately slow and clear tone.

"Aye," Jack said, simply. "If it's money you lads are after, then I'm afraid you are shit out of luck. I've only just moved into the area and I haven't sorted out a job yet."

Smyth and his accomplice sat down on the sofa across from Jack. The sofa was quite small and the two men were teetering on the larger size of forms—there wasn't a hair's width between them. Had Jack wanted to escape, he could have done so at any moment—by the time the men extracted themselves from the sofa he would be halfway across the city.

"Are you lads comfortable?" Jack asked out of mischievousness.

"We'll be grand," Smyth said, as he struggled for space on the sofa. "That you don't have a job is one of the things that we want to talk to you about."

Jack looked at him quizzically.

"Really? Are you lads from the local Jobcentre?"

"No mate, we are just a community group who would like to know why a Scot should travel to Belfast to live, especially if he has no job to go to," Smyth continued. "It doesn't exactly make a whole lot of sense to me. Maybe you could fill us in?"

Jack cleared his throat.

"And if I don't feel like filling you in? What happens then?"

"Then we go for a wee drive. The next time you are asked the question it won't be me doing the asking. Believe me mate, you really don't want that," Smyth said. The delight that flashed across his face spoke of how he loved the power that was in reality only afforded to him by men who really held power. It meant that he could act the big man without the fear of being challenged or without having to get his hands dirty.

Jack smiled, and then he sighed.

"OK, it's late lads and I'd just as soon head to bed. What is it that you want to know?"

"Who you are and why you are here?" Smyth replied.

"Martin Quinn and I'm here to find out who the hell I am," Jack answered. "My mother was Mary Quinn. She came from Belfast. From this area, so I'm told."

Smyth sat back in the sofa as best he could. He thought for a few moments.

"Mary Quinn? Never heard of her and I know everyone."

"She died during a riot twenty years ago. I was taken into care in England as she didn't have family back home to look after me. I am here to talk to anyone who might be able to tell me about my mother, or other family that I don't know about."

"Sorry for your loss," Smyth said, casually. "If your Ma lived in England, where did you get that twang from?"

"When I was being placed into care I was only a baby. I was passed from one local authority to another until I finally ended up in Scotland. I have been there ever since."

"And how do you propose to keep yourself? With no money or no job," Smyth asked.

"I have done an apprenticeship in one of the yards back home. Engineering. I was hoping that there might be something going down at the docks," Jack explained.

Smyth smiled.

"Christ Almighty man, have you been sleeping these last few years? There is no work anywhere. The shipbuilding industry is dying and any jobs there are will not be available to the likes of you," Smyth said, bitterly.

"Why? I thought everyone loved the Scots," Jack replied.

"They do alright, but with a name like Martin Quinn, being a Scot isn't going to help you."

"I don't understand," Jack protested, but he knew exactly what Smyth was hinting at.

The shipyard was located in East Belfast, a traditional Loyalist stronghold. For decades the vast majority of workers came from the area and even in the wake of new anti-discrimination laws the workforce was still mainly Protestant. The new laws, which arose out of the Civil Rights protests of the '60s, compelled employers to recruit along non-sectarian lines. However, employers were not legally obligated to protect the rights of those workers. Intimidation ensured that only the most hardened Catholic would even think about looking for a job at the shipyard. None of these issues were going to affect Jack as a job at the yard had already been arranged for him. Jack wondered if miraculously getting the job in a few weeks time would in itself raise suspicions.

"Back home you might have been a proud Scot. Over here you are nothing more than another Finnian. Your kind are not welcomed down at the docks," Smyth explained.

"If you are a wise man you will give them a different name when you go looking for work. When there was plenty of work on they allowed the odd token Catholic into the yard, but now things are tough they are running a strictly Prods only recruitment policy. Welcome to Belfast."

97

"Mmm. What do you suggest? Billy Orange," Jack quipped.

"Anything but Martin. Anything but Quinn."

"I'll bear that in mind," Jack said.

"So Martin, what do you know about your Ma. I might be able to help you track down some of your family. Or at the very least, I should be able to put you in touch with some people who knew her."

Jack leaned forward and he began to tell his story. They listened intently, making a mental note of every detail of his story so that he could be questioned on the facts of what he said at some later date in an effort to catch him out.

The Queen's Arms was his new local. Jack found it amusing that the pub was named in honour of Queen Victoria as it was located deep in the heart of a Republican area and none of the patrons held any love for the British royal family.

Jack knew that the impression of Northern Ireland portrayed on the news was never going to be quite like reality, but he was surprised at just how little the troubles impacted on the daily lives of everyday people. If it wasn't for the frequent shootings and bombings, Belfast could have been any other UK city. The army patrols were met by a torrent of abuse when they passed through the Markets area, and sometimes the verbal assault turned into a stone throwing incident. In the pub there was very little talk of the trouble outside on the streets. It was very much a community boozer—pub quizzes, charity events, stag nights and a disco every Friday night—and most importantly, there was the craic and the gossip.

One Saturday evening an old man sat down beside Jack in the pub. He was in his seventies and his hand shook as he held a pint of Guinness.

"You are Mary Quinn's boy," he said.

"Aye," Jack said, despondently. He had grown tired of the conversations about Mary Quinn. People appeared very interested in helping him find out about his mother, and many claimed that they knew someone who would definitely have known her, but none of those leads bore fruit—and that suited Jack just fine.

"I knew Mary," said the old man. "She was a lovely girl. I was so sorry to hear about her passing. I had wished better for her. I often wondered why she didn't stay away. I imagined that she would marry well and live a happy life over in England, well away from this shithole. Whatever possessed her to come back to this place, I'll never know. It held no luck for her. She should have kept well away."

He took a long sip of his drink before continuing.

"Aye, she had a poor start in life," he continued.

Another sip. A long pause. The old man leaned forward and he spoke in a low voice.

"Son, I know why you have really come back," he said. "I know some people who you should meet."

Jack looked confused. The old man leaned back in his seat before he continued to speak.

"Unless I am wrong about you? Wrong about why you have really come back to Belfast? Am I wrong?"

Jack finished his drink.

"Aye, you know why I'm really here," Jack said. "I want to avenge my mother's death."

The old man lit a cigarette and he took a long draw on it. He coughed twice.

"You can no longer avenge her death, Martin. Not in the way that you intend. The young soldier who murdered your Ma has long since gone. We never knew who he was. You could kill every Brit in Belfast and the man who killed her will still be alive. That's just the way it is. The men who I want you to meet know that. They also know that someone so blinded by hatred and revenge that they lose their head, is a danger to everyone. They do not want to work with a man like that. Do you understand what I am telling you, Martin?"

Jacked nodded his head, yes.

"Good man. If you really want in tell them that you are prepared to help the struggle in whatever way you can. You will watch the movements of the troops, or rattle tins at the pub on a Friday night. Whatever they need you to do. Show that you can be useful, but at the same time, prove to them that you are not fanatical. Do that and you will get what you really want."

Before Jack had a chance to say anything, the old man stood up. He offered a hand for Jack to shake.

"It was a pleasure to meet you Martin," he said. "And for your sainted mother's sake, I hope that you get the chance to do what we both know you need to do."

With that he was gone.

Kieran Smyth sat down beside Jack once the old man had gone.

"Who was that old bloke?" Jack asked, nodding in the direction of the man as he glad-handed his way across the room.

"That old bloke is the kind of man who could have us both killed here and now by simply nodding his head. He sure as hell wouldn't take too kindly to me telling you his name. If he had wanted you to know who he was, he would have told you. Now stop asking stupid questions and get the drinks in."

Jack smiled as he got up and walked towards the bar. He looked across the room in time to see the old man leaving the pub closely followed by two large men. The man on the right had a gun tucked into the back of his jeans, under his tight fitting jacket. The outline of the weapon was clear for all to see. As he placed his order with the young barmaid, Jack smiled—he had finally made direct contact with the terrorists.

After almost a year with no progress, Jack and his commanding officers had been about to pull the plug. In the background, unbeknownst to Jack, Commander Deeley had been rushing from one tempestuous meeting to another; calling in every favour owed to him and shamelessly exploiting any political contact he possibly could in order to keep his pet project alive.

During that time Jack had very little direct contact with his family and friends and the mission was really starting to wear him down. The chance meeting in the pub with the IRA leader had turned all of his misgivings on their head. Two days after the initial contact, Kieran came to Jack's home.

"You have been summoned," said Kieran.

"Yeah? By who?"

"By the kind of people who only summon you once."

Jack looked decidedly unimpressed as he tried to contain his excitement. Everything that he had been through over the last year had been leading up to that moment, and now that it was finally here, Jack was nervous. One wrong move at that point and he would blow it.

"Tell me something about them," Jack said. "How well do you know them?"

"I don't know them. I know of them and should tell you everything that you need to know about them."

Jack got his coat and they left. Kieran was very quiet. They crossed the border about an hour and a half after leaving Belfast. They changed cars once across the border. Two men were waiting for them in the second car. As was common for such meetings, they were blindfolded and driven in secrecy to their final destination.

Jack and Kieran dutifully obeyed the instructions. After a short drive they were pulled from the car and then marched into an old farm building. The smell of diesel assaulted Jack's nose and caused him to gag. Instinctively his highly trained mind went into overdrive as he gathered and processed as much information as he could about his current location. Fuel was often used in some of the bigger IRA bombs — that accounted for the smell, but his exact location was a complete mystery to him. He called up a map of Ireland in his mind and he calculated where he might be located given the duration of the journey and the speed that they were travelling. That area was so vast that it was beyond useless. Jack and Kieran were forced to sit down. Jack scanned the room in lazy fashion—a guilty man would not look—or so he was told. At the same time, it was one thing to cautiously gather as much information about his surroundings as he possibly could, but it was an entirely different, more deadly prospect to be seen to be gathering as much information as he possibly could. It was a balancing act for which he had no idea where the true equilibrium lay—if he seemed too interested in the men and the room that he was in they would grow suspicious, and if he acted as if he couldn't care less, they would grow even more suspicious. If he had a chance to talk to the men one on one he could very quickly work out where he should pitch that balance, but as this was an interrogation where he would do the vast majority of the talking, he was going to have to rely on their better judgement and a great deal of luck to see him through.

He had read reports on this type of meeting. Six men sat across from him. The automatic weapons were pointed at the backs of Jack and Kieran's heads. If any of the answers that they gave were not to the men's liking then there would be a knowing nod of the head; an unspoken signal to the men with the guns and it would be over. Jack had wanted to point out to the men standing behind him with their guns trained on his head that the use of automatic weapons in such a confined area could be very dangerous, but he got the impression that it wasn't the time for humour.

11

In A Mirror Darkly

"Who are you?" asked one of the men. The menace in the man's voice told of how he was not going to be happy with whatever answer Jack gave.

He struggled to strike a convincible balance between fear and innocence. He went on to repeat the story that he had learned so well before he moved to Belfast, and which had been repeated so many times since that time that there were moments when Jack almost believed the story himself. Kieran nodded his head in agreement with Jack's words every now and then; confirming that what Jack was saying at that time was the same as the story he had told him a year before, and several times since. When Jack had finished telling they took him outside. After ten minutes he was brought back in and then he was told to have a seat.

"We have looked into your story in some detail over the past year," one of the men began. "There are a few things that don't add up. Maybe you could help us with them?"

"I'll do my best," Jack replied.

"You will need to do your best, Martin. You will need to do your very best," Kieran said. "Like your life depends on it."

There was another dramatic pause as Jack was left to soak in the pressure.

"We have many volunteers working on the mainland," the spokesman for the group continued. "And they have been working tirelessly over these last few months trying to find out as much about you as they possibly can."

"And what did they find out?" Jack asked, with only a trace of concern in his tone.

"See, that's the thing. They found out nothing. You have no history with the police, you have never claimed any benefits and we haven't met a single person who has ever met you. In short Martin, apart from your Social Services records when you were a baby, you don't seem to exist."

Jack looked worried. He formed words of protest but he couldn't get them to leave his mouth. After all the careful plans and preparations, could it really end like this? Did Deeley and the other thinkers within the service not go deep enough with his cover story? Were they so arrogant as to believe that the IRA would not probe the background of a potential new recruit to the nth degree? As he sat back in the chair and sighed, Jack concluded that the IRA man sitting across from him was bluffing.

"I don't know what to tell you," Jack said. "I have claimed benefits many times. Hell, I even claimed benefits when I first moved to Belfast. I don't know why your people weren't able to find those records, but I can assure you, they do exist."

"My people are thorough," snapped the man. "They could not find any records. That tells me those records did not exist. You are either lying to us or you just happen to be the most unlucky man on the island of Ireland at this moment in time."

Jack went to lean forwards in an effort to stress his case more strenuously, but as he moved the gunman standing behind him pulled Jack back into his chair. The barrel of the gun was now pressed firmly against the back of his head.

"Tell us who you really are and I will bring this to an end as painlessly as possible. Lie to me one more time and I will put you through the kind of the suffering that the Devil himself would be afeared of. Tell us who you really are!" he snapped.

Jack remained as calm as a man staring at the end of his own life could be.

"I have told you who I am. I have told you why I have come to Ireland. You know why I'm in this room. If you want to torture me I will tell you what you want to hear, the only problem is it will be one hundred percent bullshit. There is nothing more that I can say to you. If you think I am lying, then kill me."

There was a short pause.

"Last chance. Tell us who you are!"

Jack remained tight lipped. The gunman standing behind him pressed the gun more firmly against his skull, forcing his head downwards. Jack said nothing more. The gunman readied his weapon for firing. Jack grimaced at the sound of metal on metal as the gunman worked the cocking handle.

"Who the hell are you!"

Jack held his ground. He knew that his fate had already been decided and that there wasn't a thing that he could say to the men to change the outcome. If they had really suspected that he was an enemy agent then the interrogation would have been a lot more hands on.

"Martin Quinn," Jack said eventually, in answer to the question that had been put to him. "Martin Thomas Quinn."

"Who sent you!" yelled the man, as he jumped to his feet. The man pulled out a pistol that had been tucked into the back of his jeans. He grabbed the table by a corner and flung it to one side—one of the legs fell off on impact and it tumbled across the floor. The man grabbed Jack by the back of the head and then he pressed the gun against his forehead. He saw weakness in Jack's words and with one more push all of his defences would be down.

"Who sent you!" he repeated.

Jack did not answer the question.

"I'm going to count to three and if you haven't told us who sent you by the time I reach three, you are a dead man. Now, tell us, who sent you?"

Jack looked directly into the man's eyes. He remained silent.

"One..."

Jack remained silent.

"Two..."

Jack remained silent.

"Three..."

Jack remained silent, but he closed his eyes as he prepared for the end.

"Enough!" a voice called from one of the adjoining rooms. The man holding the gun to Jack's head stepped back. He was putting his gun back into his jeans when Jack opened his eyes.

The old man from the Queen's Arms walked into the room. He quickly moved across to Jack.

"I am sorry that you had to go through all that," said the man. "But we had to be sure. I hope you can understand?"

Jack said nothing. There was anger written across his face.

"The Brits have sent several agents to infiltrate our group in the past few years. These methods may seem a bit extreme but the life of every man in this room depends on keeping those spies out. I make no apology for that. I will give you a few minutes to collect yourself together. We have decided to give you a chance to serve your country," said the man.

The man walked away from Jack and he chatted loudly with the other men in the room as if the set-up was nothing out of the ordinary. They were talking about a new golf course that was being built outside Dundalk. Jack sat pensively as if contemplating what he meant by serve your country, but his ears were firmly honed in on the conversation that the men were having. From what Jack could glean from the slow drip of information that was being knocked around the room, the IRA had moved on from merely intimidating businessmen—through ownership of the golf course they had become businessmen. The old man returned to stand in front of Jack.

"A few introductions. I am Cathal Polin. The rest of the

lads will be introduced to you if, or when it is necessary. I will be your main contact back in the North. I will let you know about your assignments, either directly, or through Kieran. Though to be honest, the way things are at the moment, it will probably be through Kieran. The Brits have been watching me round the clock lately. It was a mighty hassle to get clear of them long enough to make it down here. Once they realise that I did slip through their net they will be sure to put even more surveillance in place.

"We are going to send you out on a mission in Belfast. Your target will be an off duty soldier. He is seeing a local. She will lead the soldier to you and you will kill him. How do you feel about that? Are you really ready to serve?"

"Yes," Jack said simply.

As he was driven back to Belfast he had a lot to think about. This was going to be difficult and only hoped that someone in London didn't decide that the death of a soldier was a small price to pay for getting Jack admitted to the IRA.

Back in Belfast, the waiting game started again. Jack decided that it would be best not to say anything about the mission, not even to Kieran. If someone who he knew brought it up specifically then that was different, but he would keep mum in order to stay alive.

Although he had been expecting it, when he was finally called in to carry out the murder it did take him by surprise. It didn't leave him with a lot of time to make the proper preparations. The gun he was to use was left with him so that he could familiarise himself with the weapon. He got a message through to his handler and he arranged for blanks to be sent to Jack's house. The soldier was identified—the girl in question was a regular at the pub and she had been coerced into setting the trap.

During a casual conversation one night at the Crown, Jack had mentioned that he was a big motorcycle enthusiast. What to him was just a random conversation was taken in and processed by those around him. That skill, born out of his interest in bikes, was to be put to good use.

Dressed in black leathers and wearing a helmet with a tinted visor, Jack found himself riding through the rain-soaked streets of Belfast late one night. The gun was tucked into the jacket of his leathers.

The attack went like clockwork. He drove up to the soldier and the girl. He fired six "shots" into his back. The soldier hit the ground and played dead. The girl jumped on the bike behind him and they drove off to safety. The media was fed a false story and soon Jack was a hero in his adopted community. It could not have been any easier and the people in the IRA who really mattered were very impressed with him.

He was even offered an engineering job by one of his passengers. The job was in the Republic and he told Deeley about it—there was glint in his commander's eye when Jack spoke of the job offer. His accent and passport meant that the troops manning the border patrols on the Northern side of the border rarely asked questions.

The bombings and shootings, both in Northern Ireland, and with increasing frequency on the Mainland, continued with no signs of letting up. He had come so close to being discovered, to being killed, and the danger that he had put himself in appeared to have been for nothing. Once again his thoughts turned to life after the mission and once again he set in his mind to call an end to the operation once and for all. Even if Deeley said no to his request to wind up the mission, there was a lot that Jack could do to make that happen, if he so desired. He could take Kieran to a police station and tell him the truth, before disappearing into the fortified safety of the building. Events once again got in the way of his plans—Ireland had not quite finished with Jack.

12

Empire

There was a lull in all activity surrounding Jack following the so-called shooting. Initially Jack had assumed this was because the security forces would be on a higher state of alert, but after some time he got the idea in his head that he had done something wrong. As time wore on he grew even more concerned as a mist of paranoia crept into his thoughts. Every stranger that he met at work or out on the street; every car the back-fired; every knock on his door—they all spelled doom for him. In fact, he felt under a lot less pressure when he was sitting in a chair deep in the Irish countryside with a gun pressed against the back of his head.

Had someone from the organisation been watching the events surrounding the staged killing? Were they simply waiting for the opportunity to put him down? It was a very real possibility. He should have been more careful. The interview process did not begin and end that night across the border—the interview process for someone like him would never end.

The July and August marching season brought turmoil to the streets of Belfast, but as the paramilitaries on both sides were heavily involved in this annual knock-about, Jack could breathe easy for a short time. The attacks and counter attacks, the incursions into enemy territory, and the police and army on every street corner acting as referee—this was a perfect distraction, behind which he could move with relative ease.

Making contact with Deeley proved straightforward

during the marching season. He simply tagged along to a riot, and then he put himself in a position where he would get arrested—throwing a brick normally did it—had he opted for a petrol bomb he ran the risk of being shot. In an emergency Deeley would call him at his house but the line was not secure and there were restrictions placed on what they could say. In one of the police stations or army bases, Jack was free to chat freely over a secure line, or in person.

"I'm not asking to end the mission," Jack said. "I just want to go home for a few days to see my family."

Deeley glared at him.

"We discussed that at the outset, Jack," Deeley began. His voice was measured and it did not reflect the anger held in his eyes. "Do you really want to put at risk all that you have achieved?"

"I don't see how going back home will do that," Jack protested. "They know that I have friends back in Scotland."

Deeley, sensing that there was no way that he could get Jack to back down, and that if he pulled rank on him his very resourceful asset might just find a way to get what he wanted anyway, decided that the only way to continue with the operation was to give Jack what he wanted. This was a courtesy that he did not extend to many men under his command.

"Jack, I will see what I can do. The mission must come first, but if the opportunity arises to bring you back home for a couple of days, I will make it happen."

This time Jack needed more. It had been an age since he last saw his mother and on that occasion the old woman did not look well.

"I need for you to commit to this, sir," Jack said, forcefully.

"Be reasonable Jack. It is not simply a matter of bringing you back home on the next flight out of Belfast. Hell, the security surrounding your return home would be tighter than that surrounding a Presidential visit."

"What?" snapped Jack.

"For Christ's sake Jack, you will leave a paper trail from here to Glasgow. A paper trail that could be intercepted and followed at any stage. You know this as well as I do. You buy a ticket for your flight or for the ferry here in Belfast. Do you know the person that you are buying the ticket from? Can you be certain that they are not associated with the IRA? And when you do get back to Scotland they have agents there too, just waiting for you to arrive so that they can follow you. Bottom line, there is too much going on elsewhere and we simply can't afford the agents needed to baby-sit you."

"Don't be so dramatic, sir. I have worked with these people. I have lived among them and I have killed for them."

Deeley stood up from behind the desk. He was not accustomed to having his decisions questioned.

"But are you prepared to die for them?" Deeley asked. "That is what it would come to if they follow you to Scotland without us running interference. Like I said, I will see what I can do. Above and beyond that, I can do no more."

Deeley moved to the door of the interview room. He turned to face Jack before leaving.

"Second Presbyterian, 11:30 on Sunday morning," Deeley said.

"What?" quizzed Jack.

"Last Sunday morning, I watched your mother as she went into the Presbyterian Church on Duke Street. She was looking well."

As Deeley opened the door and left he room Jack felt slightly confused and a little apprehensive. Did Deeley mean to reassure him or intimidate him? A warm pulse of fear and anger rushed through his body and it left him feeling a little sickly.

Deeley made contact in November. He spoke with Jack over the phone in his house. That rarely happened and Jack's immediate reaction was that something was wrong with his mother or sister.

"Mr Quinn?" Deeley asked down the line, for the benefit of any eavesdropper.

"This is Martin Quinn."

"Mr Quinn, I am calling from the Inland Revenue with regard to your tax statement for the last year. There are just a couple of things I would like to confirm. Would you have a few moments?"

"Sure, fire away," Jack replied.

"You are down on our records as having been on unemployment benefit and housing assistance for 6 months of last year?"

"That sounds about right."

"OK. Your tax code was calculated based on you being in full-time employment for the entire year. That is our mistake. The good news is you will be getting a little money returned to you. I will carry out my final calculation and you should get a cheque in the post in the next few days."

"That's fantastic news," Jack said, as he tried to sound suitably excited.

"OK sir. Are there any questions that you would like to ask me?" Deeley enquired.

"No mate, that's grand. I am just thinking about how I am going to spend my wee windfall."

"OK then sir. Thank you for your time, and please accept our apologies for the mistake."

"No worries," Jack added, before replacing the receiver.

Jack smiled. He had been trained to seek out the main keywords in that kind of conversation. Deeley wasn't saying that Jack was going home to Scotland, but he was saying that Jack should look out for a letter in the post. That in itself was a good thing—at least Deeley was trying to make it happen.

A letter arrived at his home in Belfast a few days later informing him that a woman who had once looked after him in care for several years had just died. As pretences for a return to the mainland went it wasn't terribly sophisticated, but Jack was all too aware that the less complicated the lie, the more chance there was for successes. Deeley had impressed that fact on him again and again and it was a lesson that Jack kept close to his heart at all times. It was the main reason why he hadn't gone into any long and winding stories when he was being interrogated in the South. He made arrangements to return to Scotland to attend the funeral. A foster carer had indeed died in the small Scottish town of Cully, twenty miles outside of Edinburgh and Jack did attend the funeral—they could never be certain who was watching and even with his cover firmly established, things could change very quickly. Deeley did not make contact with Jack at the funeral.

Jack introduced himself at the funeral as someone from Social Services. He had toyed with the idea of posing as one of the kids who the deceased had cared for but he decided against that idea in the end. If people took too much interest in him then it would only be a matter of time before he betrayed himself. There were certain to be other children there who had genuinely been cared for by the dead woman—what if one of them recalled something deeply personal that only a child who had been cared for by the woman would know— do you remember what she used to say at breakfast? We used to love visiting with her—what was the name of the village where we used to stay? Too many questions; too much risk. And what about her immediate family—surely one of them would remember Jack if he truly had been cared for by her?

The service was short and sweet. The minister, though Presbyterian, did not linger too long during his sermon. Sin bad; no sin good. The preacher was young and although he didn't impart impatience during the service, the speed with which he brought proceedings to an end did give the impression that he had better things to do.

It was as they were lowering the coffin into the grave when Jack noticed someone standing by the edge of the main crowd. At first Jack only gave the woman a quick glance—

perhaps she was one of the many young people who the dead woman had once cared for? The names of those children had all been listed during the service in the church, after the names of her own son and daughter and her husband. On watching the woman a little more carefully Jack noticed that there was something very odd about how she was behaving. She was not so much interested in what was going on by the side of the grave as she was in the people in attendance. It wasn't that unusual that someone should be checking out who was crying; what they were wearing, and so on, but this was somehow different, almost obsessive. It was an odd way for her to act, Jack thought.

The paranoia generated by his current assignment had left him feeling a little on edge and to begin with he simply dismissed his concern as being nothing more than a stress related overreaction. The woman may have come from a troubled background, and even though the preacher had done a mighty job of portraying the foster mother as a saint, Jack knew that there were some kids in the care system that even the most saintly could do nothing for. Perhaps this woman had been one such child? Perhaps the dead woman had tried and tried and tried but in the end she had to give up on her?

He continued to watch the woman for another ten minutes. She was still behaving in the same way. Jack shifted back and forth on the spot. There was something more—she seemed familiar. Had he been watching her so intently that his brain was generating a false sense of recognition? There was certainly something not quite right with the woman and in that moment Jack decided that he was going to try to find out what that something was. He only hoped that she didn't turn on him violently and generate the kind of public scene that he had been so carefully trying to avoid.

Cautiously Jack began to edge his way around the outside of the crowd towards the woman. She was standing in the shade of an ancient oak tree, though Jack considered her position to be born out of a desire to keep a low profile rather than a genuine attempt to seek protection from the sun. From the somewhat random way the woman was scanning the people by the graveside it appeared to Jack that she was not certain who it was that she was looking for—perhaps she was using her mind's eye to age people so that their appearance from then matched up with the appearance of those now standing in front of her? So preoccupied was she with her search that she didn't notice as Jack closed in on her position as he paced out a huge, sweeping arc that would terminate at the far side of the oak, just in behind the woman.

"It was a big turn-out," Jack said, when he was only yards from the woman.

The woman spun around quickly to face Jack. There was a look of surprise and concern on her face.

"Yes," she said, simply.

That one word was enough for Jack. Even though she spoke in a perfect English accent, it was an accent from early British cinema, or straight off the BBC World Service. Even more than that; it was a well rehearsed accent, and one that Jack could spot as a fake straight away. He had spent enough time in the company of Russians to pick out their affectations. She was a spy.

Jack smiled at her.

"How did you know the deceased?" Jack asked.

"Eh, I used to work with her," explained the woman.

"I see. And are you not going to go over to introduce yourself to the family?"

"Perhaps later. For now, I think that they have enough people to cope with."

Jack looked back at the crowd and then he return his gaze to the woman.

"Where did you work with her?" he asked.

"A Charity shop in town. Every Saturday morning."

Jack smile again. The woman began to move away ever so slowly as she continued to talk.

"So, how did you know her?" she asked.

"I work for Social Services. I have supervised some of the kids placed with her."

"Aww. I see. You look so young to be a social worker."

"Case manager," Jack corrected her.

"Sorry. Case manager."

"Are you sure that you don't want to take a walk over to say hello to the family? I am certain that they would be delighted to see you."

"Not right now. It could be a little awkward. I used to date her son. I'm not certain that he would want to see me at this time."

Jack looked over towards the grave. To his surprise the grave was now out of sight, hid behind a small hill, on top of which sat the oak. He hadn't noticed that they had moved so far in such a short time.

"I think that we ought to head back in the direction of the grave, even if you do not intend to go over to shake hands," Jack said.

"There was one other thing that I was wondering about," Jack continued.

"Yes?"

"Exactly which part of Russia are you originally from?"

Jack couldn't be sure when she had done it—it could have been when he was looking at the people by the graveside, or it could have been when he was scanning the graveyard for any further odd looking individuals as they walked down the hill; but whenever it had happened, the end result was the same. The short, thick branch that she used like a club made contact with the side of him head—his vision went dark for a moment and he fell to his knees. He shook it off. When he looked up he saw the woman disappearing in through the front door of the church. Jack pulled himself up off the ground and he began to hobble in the direction of the church.

Dazed and sore, Jack threw his shoulder against the heavy

wooden door of the church. The door opened, but it didn't exactly fly off its hinges like in the movies. The tiled floor of the vestibule was spoiled by a trail of muddy footprints leading to a staircase on the left hand side. The staircase led to an upper gallery that was used on those occasions when the main body of the church was full. As he ascended the stairs he reached into the jacket of his suit and pulled out the small pistol that had been left for him in the bottom drawer of the unit in his hotel room. When he found the gun he had smiled — when he was in Ireland he really needed a gun, but he was forbidden from carrying one, but now that he was back in Scotland, where it was safe, they were happy to provide him with a weapon.

His hand locked around the handle of the gun and he slipped it out of its hiding place. The spiral staircase was one big blind corner, from the first to the last step, and he moved in a very careful fashion. Jack's vision was almost fully restored by the time he reached the gallery. The pews sloped downward towards a solid rail at the front. The staircase was the only way in and out of the gallery. She was trapped. All Jack had to do was to stand by the door and wait. Sooner or later she would have to come out. Jack sat down on a seat next to the door and he waited. Five minutes. Ten minutes. Twenty minutes. Not a sound. Jack began to doubt himself. Perhaps the footprints had been a diversion? The Russians were very clever individuals and Russian spies were simply genius.

After thirty minutes someone entered the church. They walked around for a few minutes and then left. The heavy door closed behind them and Jack clearly heard a key turning as the door was locked.

"We can play this game all day, if you like," Jack announced. "But sooner or later you will have to come out."

There was no response.

"I only want to talk."

No response.

"OK. We can do this the hard way."

Jack slipped his left hand into his outside jacket pocket and he produced a silencer. He fixed the device to the end of his gun. Jack stood up; he aimed randomly at one of the pews, and then fired. The dry, highly varnished wood exploded as the bullet passed through it. Jack paused. Still no response. He fired twice in quick succession.

"OK," she yelled, from somewhere at the front of the gallery. "I'm coming out."

"Slowly if you don't mind, sweetheart. Someone just hit me in the face and I'm still a bit shaky on it. I would hate for my gun to go off accidentally."

Like an island goddess she rose up from behind the front row. The thick stick was still in her hands. In an unspoken gesture of acquiescence she threw her makeshift weapon onto the floor. Jack suppressed a smile. What the hell did she think she was doing, Jack thought. Why was she out on an assignment without a weapon? It didn't make sense. She was playing him.

"Thank you," Jack said. "Now if you would be so good as to throw your gun onto the floor as well."

"I don't have a gun," she said.

"Please. Fool me once, shame on me, fool me twice... Not bloody likely. Gun. Now. On the floor."

She slowly pulled up her dress and removed the small pistol from the holster that was strapped to her left thigh. She threw the weapon into the aisle.

"Happy?" she snapped.

"For now," Jack replied. "Slowly make your way up to me."

She paused for a moment before walking towards Jack. Jack indicated that she should take a seat by pointing with his gun. She complied.

"Isn't this a lot more civilised than fighting," Jack said.

She remained silent.

"OK then. Let's start at the beginning," Jack said. "I am not going to believe a word of what you tell me, but I suppose we have to play the game anyway. Let's start with the basics. Why are you here?"

She cleared her throat.

"I am here for you," she said.

Jack looked at her quizzically.

"For me? What the hell do you mean by that?"

"I know who you are Jack. I know why you are here. I am here to keep an eye on you. You know the story."

"Mmm, not exactly sweetheart. There is no possible way that you could know that I would be here today."

"And yet, here I am."

Jack jumped to his feet. He pointed his gun at her forehead.

"Start making sense," he said. "Or would you like me to tell the preacher to get another plot ready?"

She smiled at him. As she did a flash of recognition raced through Jack's mind. It was like the words of a poorly remembered song, or the face of an old school acquaintance—familiar, yet too distant to be placed.

"I know you," Jack said. "I have seen you somewhere before."

She smiled again.

"Who the hell are you?"

"Think of me as your guardian angel. At least when you are in the UK. I have missed you this past year. Though I have kept in touch with your mother and sister."

Her words filled him with fear and rage all at once. He pressed the gun against her forehead.

"This is the last time that I am going to ask. Who the hell are you!"

"I have been watching you from day one," she said. "I was there when you were being trained. I was there when you left on assignment. You ask me who I am, yet you already know."

He did know who she was but the fact that she confirmed

his suspicions somehow made it all seem more real and dangerous. Jack was so sure that he had been careful and he was so confident in the abilities of the service to protect him and his family. If he squeezed the trigger he would eliminate one Soviet spy, but how long would it be before they had another agent in place to pick up where she left off? He stepped back.

"Get the hell out of here," he said.

She looked at him with confusion as if she thought that he might be playing some kind of cruel game.

"What?" she asked. "You are letting me go?"

"Yes. Now get the hell out of here before I change my mind."

She turned to get the gun.

"No you don't. Leave the gun."

She smiled and then walked past Jack. As she passed him he caught a glancing side profile of her. This was enough. He knew where he had seen her before. She had been sitting in a car as he left the meeting in London where he had learned about his assignment in Ireland.

Jack followed her down the spiralling staircase to the vestibule. She walked up to the door. It was locked. She turned to Jack for help and quickly jumped to one side when she saw him standing with the gun in his hand. Jack fired three times. Each bullet hit the target—just to the right of the keyhole. She pulled on the door. It opened this time. Jack stood by the open doorway as he watched her disappear across the churchyard. Once she was out of sight, Jack left the church. As he walked away from the church his head was filled with all kinds of uncertainties. How much did the Russians know about what he was doing in Ireland? Was his family in any danger? Would they, one day, use threats to his family against him?

He stayed at the Grand Hotel in central Edinburgh. Deeley was booked into the hotel as well and they met up at two in the morning that night. The meeting took place in Jack's bedroom.

"You have made excellent progress," said Deeley. "Much better than we had hoped for. We have another mission and we believe you are in an excellent position to help us with it."

Lighting a cigarette and waiting for Deeley to continue, Jack was feeling mildly frustrated at that moment as it seemed that the better he performed, the more they wanted to punish him. They were playing Russian roulette with his life and the only way he was getting out was if he was killed by the IRA or if he blew his own cover when it was safe to do so. The woman in the church had completely shifted his focus back to Scotland and the need to protect his family from his way of life.

"We have been fighting this war against the IRA for a long time, yet we know so little about how the organisation works. They would have us believe that it is comprised of independent cells which take part in their own missions, without being sanctioned by the leadership. In fact, they would have us believe that there is no real leadership—not in the traditional sense. When you look at the attacks over the past year or two, there does not appear to be any joined up thinking. Sometimes a warning is given before a bomb goes off, sometimes there is no warning, and even a second device is detonated as people try to escape. There appears to be no logic to their methods, as if these attacks are coming from very different groups. I believe this is what they want us to think. If one attack goes terribly wrong and women and children are killed, they can lay the blame at the feet of a small, unaccountable group within the organisation. If a man is captured, the flow of information he can provide is limited to the cell he belongs to. You have been driving the men we believe are leading the organisation in Northern Ireland to meet with the leaders in the South. We need to know who those men are and we need to know how the decisions they make are relayed to the ground troops. The job that you were offered would put you at the very heart of the organisation. We want you to take that job."

Deeley was completely calm when he went over his expectations from the mission, as if what he was asking was no more complicated than getting a kitten out of a tree. The file that Deeley produced contained pictures of the main players, as far as the intelligence services could ascertain, as well as a detailed breakdown of the IRA's business interests. It was a massive global enterprise that in total would have rivalled many of the FTSE 100 companies.

As Jack sat on the edge of the bed looking over the documents it occurred to him that this Irish terror group, born out of British imperialism from the most humble of beginnings, was now a true industrial military machine. The Army part of the IRA name was now much more than an often mocked symbol. With such power and wealth the organisation was capable of a war of attrition and annihilation. Jack's blood ran cold as a chilling thought occurred to him—the atrocities of recent years carried out by the IRA were not the best they could do; those atrocities were the IRA showing restraint.

Before the meeting with Deeley, Jack had drawn a sketch of the woman from the church. He had intended to tell Deeley that he was now compromised and that he would have to withdraw from the assignment in Ireland. His true intention was to protect his family. But the information that Deeley presented to him proved just how important his cover was. It would take another agent a year to reach the same position, if they even made it that far, and in that time the IRA could kill hundreds.

"Do you have any questions?" Deeley asked.

Jack paused.

"No. I think you have made it clear just how important this is. I will do my very best to bring the organisation down."

"Good man. You really have been doing outstanding work. Don't think that it has gone unnoticed higher up the chain of command."

Deeley moved to the door of Jack's bedroom.

"Sir," Jack said. "This is getting pretty serious. If I am discovered my family will be in real danger. I want you to put more security on them. Please."

"Of course," Deeley said, passively. "It is the very least that we can do. You have my word, Jack. No harm will come to them."

Deeley left. The next few days that Jack spent with his family were precious to him. He treated every moment like it was their last. As he left Edinburgh for the boat back to Ireland he felt numb. There was so much that he needed to do. The lives of countless innocent men, women and children depended on him, and it was not an easy burden to live with. He was also very aware of the personal decision he had just reached—he was risking the life of his mother and sister in order to save the lives of strangers.

13

Undiscovered Country

By the time Jack returned to Northern Ireland he was feeling a little more secure and confident, but only a little. The biggest mission of his life had started the moment that he left the hotel room back in Edinburgh and like a runaway train, there was simply too much momentum for Jack to stop it even if he had wanted to. When he was standing in line waiting to disembark at Belfast harbour, news of a massive car bomb in the mid-Ulster town of Banbridge was beginning to filter through. When he got back to his house he tuned into BBC Radio Ulster for an update. Jeremy Paxman, a young English reporter who was making a name for himself at the BBC in Belfast, was at the scene. Paxman was reserved and somewhat stoic and he had a way of making the local politicians look silly by slyly reflecting the idiocy of their tribal ideology back at them. Jack respected Paxman's journalistic integrity as he never pandered to the politicians,no matter how scary they were or how many gunmen they had at their disposal. As he listened to Paxman updating the studio from the scene of the explosion, he knew that it was bad—there was emotion in Paxman's voice.

"The facade of the main shopping area has been reduced to bricks and mortar. Masonry that had not been destroyed at the time of the blast is now falling away from the twisted metal skeleton that remains, making the job of the emergency services that much more difficult," Paxman reported. "It has been almost two hours since the bomb went off and there are still ghostly men, women and children wandering the main street. Most are covered head to toe in a fine white dust, and some have blood stained faces from superficial head wounds that the first responders have checked out, before turning their attention to higher priority victims. From where I stand I can see several bodies covered with white sheets. Two of those sheets are covering the bodies of children."

By the time the late evening news came on the death toll was confirmed as six women, three men and three children. As Jack watched the devastation it made him feel angry. That was nothing compared to the anger he felt when the political representatives of those who carried out the attack appeared in front of the cameras and refused to condemn the atrocity. Jack's resolve stiffened as he turned in for the night. He had a job to do and it was a job that no one else was able to do.

Through his contacts in Belfast he got a message through to the leadership in the South, and before he had time to say goodbye to those people in the city who thought of him as their friend, he was crossing the border in South Armagh. That part of the county was officially still part of the UK, but the reality was the IRA ruled every aspect of life in South Armagh, from who was allowed to set up home in the area to acting as the local police force, courts service and prison service. Their prison service was the envy of the world— zero prisoners—minor crimes were dealt with through punishment beatings; major crimes normally ended with the guilty person being executed.

The IRA men and women of South Armagh were amongst some of the organisation's most fanatical volunteers. The IRA and its honour code were something to be respected and feared. It was respected by the people from the area like a religion, and anyone who came into their area was expected to follow the code without question. The region was known to the people of Northern Ireland as bandit country, and for good reason. The terrorists controlled all aspects of life in South Armagh. The army had bases in the area but they were there as an act of defiance towards the gunmen rather than serving any useful security function. Soldiers and all supplies had to be flown in and out of the bases by helicopters and foot patrols were only every carried out when reinforcements were called in from all over the UK. Such patrols were carefully staged media events that served no useful purpose—they were supposed to prove to the public that the government was in control, but they fooled no one. The IRA arranged their own publicity stunts for the cameras—masked man setting up checkpoints and asking motorists for identification—a sinister shadow of the legitimate patrols that the army carried out. They also released videos of training camps and the volunteers playing war games in the South Armagh countryside.

For the most part the entire area was independent of UK and the Republic of Ireland. It was run by a handful of men and woman who controlled every aspect of the lives of those under their control. All indications of British rule had been erased—from the crown on telephone boxes and post offices, to the unmarked postal vans that were driven nervously along the narrow country roads. When national papers criticised an IRA atrocity a decree would be issued to shops in the area to stop selling that paper. For any business that defied the order the consequences were swift and devastating—the lucky business owners had their shops burned to the ground; the unlucky ones were subjected to a ruthless beating or worse. Girls who stopped to talk to the young soldiers on patrol would be taken from their beds in the middle of the night and interrogated—if they were fortunate they would have their hair cut off as a punishment; the unlucky girls received beatings, and in one case the beating was so severe that the girl went into renal failure.

The official border crossings were well manned and very secure. Every vehicle crossing from the South was subjected to a search—another pointless exercise to reassure the public given the fact that the terrorists never used the official crossings. Some farms had land that stretched across the invisible frontier, and in one ridiculous case the front of a house was in the north, and the back of the house in the south. The porous nature of the border became very familiar to Jack in the time that he spent with the IRA men from the south. They were a strange breed compared to those who he dealt with in Belfast. The Belfast volunteers were quite relaxed and the war they were fighting was badly organised and a little haphazard. If it wasn't for the deadly nature of what they were trying to achieve, there was something decidedly comical about their campaign—one classic example being the incident where a miscommunication led to the getaway car being burnt before they had actually got away. Although the consequences of their campaign were devastating, it was fought with inefficiency and blind luck. Their comrades in the south were better organised; much more ruthless and very clever. In the war with the UK the southern branch was rarely mentioned—very few of them were ever caught, and those who were caught never gave anything away and they always denied membership of the IRA—by contrast some of the Belfast brigade would shout IRA slogans when being led away by the police. They were behind the majority of the "spectacular" atrocities and they often regarded their northern comrades as enthusiastic, if somewhat ham-fisted, amateurs. When they were selecting a candidate to join their inner circle they always had a specific role in mind. Bravery and commitment to the cause were not terribly important as Republican housing estates all across Belfast and beyond were filled to bursting with young men who met those basic requirements. More important was intelligence and the ability to mislead and adapt when faced with the pressure that the British state was certain to apply to them. The ability to be caught with a smoking gun in your hand and a dead man lying at your feet and still deny all knowledge of how he died was the kind of person they were looking for.

Jack filled an entirely different need for this ruthless band of revolutionaries—he could give them access. No one would think twice about letting a Scot into areas where he ought not to be. Even the police and army would not question him if they found him scouting a possible target. Army intelligence had officers entrenched all over Ireland and many of those officers were recruited from the Scottish regiments. Jack experienced this for himself on the first evening that he crossed the border to start his new job. He followed the map that had been hastily drawn for him on the back of an envelope in a Belfast bar—he had been reassured that the road that he had been instructed to use would be clear. Cutbacks in the Ministry of Defence budget meant that it was no longer possible to man every minor road and every dirt track that crossed into the Republic. As Jack snaked his way along a suspiciously pockmarked trail he came across an army patrol. A red light moving up and down in the darkness was the signal to stop. The lights of the car illuminated a temporary sign by the side of the road that read, "Stop! Checkpoint. Turn off your lights and stop your engine."

"Do you have any form of identification, sir?" the young soldier asked Jack, through the open window.

Jack fumbled around in the glove box of the Cortina he was driving until he located the driving licence which contained photographic identification—another uniquely Northern Irish daily routine.

"Here you go," Jack said, as he handed the licence over to the soldier.

The soldier barely looked at the licence before handing it back to Jack.

"You have a nice evening, sir," said the soldier.

The young man winked at Jack as he drove away. Jack was speechless. It was not hard for him to understand why they were losing the war. If he was a terrorist he had not been challenged, and if he was undercover then the wink from the young soldier would have just betrayed him to the IRA spies who would surely be watching the checkpoint from the surrounding countryside.

As he continued on his journey into the Irish countryside he did so with one eye on the map in his head and one eye on what would be waiting for him. Cathal Polin would be there to make the introductions and that too presented Jack with mixed feelings—he was a familiar face, but he was also a very dangerous and perceptive individual who knew Jack better than the other men and who would pick up on anything suspicious. It was a high stakes game and even a small mistake could prove fatal.

His journey took him just south of Dundalk — a well known Republican stronghold. There was a much more direct route to his final destination but the main road between Newry in the north, and Dundalk in the south was heavily patrolled by the army and the police. It wasn't uncommon for the security forces on that route to set up several checkpoints in a series and if Jack made it through all of those checkpoints unchallenged then the men he was going to meet certainly would have a few questions for him.

Half an hour out of Dundalk Jack saw the familiar sight of the red light waving up and down. Automatically he reduced his speed as he approached the checkpoint and then he turned off his engine and headlights when he brought the car to a stop. A man approached. Jack moved to wind the window down but before he did there was a knock on the window. The sound was not knuckle on glass—it was metal on glass. Jack looked up to see the barrel of a Soviet made Kalashnikov pointing at him. He was not an expert on weapons by any means, but he knew that no legitimate security forces overtly used this weapon.

"Get out of the car," ordered the gunman.

Jack calmly obeyed. The gunman spun Jack around and then he pushed him against the car. Professionally he patted Jack down as he checked for weapons. He found nothing.

"Move," said the gunman, pointing with his gun.

Jack began to walk away from his car in the direction that the gunman was indicating. In the darkness, a short distance along the road, a dark blue Land Rover was waiting for them. The back door to the vehicle opened and Jack got in. Two masked men with handguns were waiting for him in the back of the Land Rover. Jack didn't offer any kind of resistance; he didn't even try to explain who he was—they knew who he was—this was their game and there was nothing that he could possibly say to them that would cause them to play that game in a different way.

There was no bag over his head this time, a fact which Jack used to convince himself that these men trusted him significantly more than the men who had conducted the first interrogation he had been through in the south. He struggled to keep a lid on a second, more devastating thought—they didn't cover his eyes this time around because they knew that this was a one way trip—he wouldn't live to tell anyone what he saw.

Before long Jack found himself in another derelict building somewhere in the Irish countryside. A man stood behind him with a gun aimed at his head and a three man interrogation committee sat across from Jack. A dirty table separated the prisoner from his interrogators. One of the men offered Jack a cigarette. Jack lit the cigarette and he took a long draw. He was not a big fan of smoking but it somehow seemed impolite to refuse.

"You were at a checkpoint earlier," one of the men began. "The soldier let you pass without challenging you."

Jack sucked on the cigarette. He blew the smoke out slowly.

"That isn't exactly what happened. I was challenged. He asked me for identification. I showed him my driving licence."

"A quick look at a driving licence isn't what I would call a full scale interrogation," replied the man.

"What can I tell you," Jack said. "That's what the man asked me for and that's what I gave him. Should I have asked him to search the car?"

"See, that's the bit that confuses us. The ten cars that passed through the checkpoint before you were all stopped and searched. And then you drive up and in no time at all you are driving on through without so much as a word. Can you see how we might be a little confused?"

Jack took another long draw on the cigarette.

"I understand what you are saying but I am not in a position to give you an answer," Jack protested. "The only one who can tell you why the Brit let me through is standing back at checkpoint. Why don't you go back and ask him?"

The men looked at one another for a moment.

"There is more going on here than you are telling us," the man continued. "Who are you and why did that soldier let you pass so easily?"

Jack smiled.

"For Christ sake, can we get this bullshit over with?" Jack snapped. "You know exactly who I am. If you thought that there was anything odd about what happened at the checkpoint then you and I both know that I would be dead already. So please, cut the amature dramatics. Get Cathal in here so that we get this show on the road."

The men looked at one another again. The man behind Jack cocked his weapon.

"You really are a confident bastard," said the man.

Jack smiled again.

"But before you get too damn confident, just keep this in mind. I will be watching your every move. I will listen to every conversation that you have and I will look into every person who you talk to. If I think for one moment that there is something not quite right I will take great pleasure in putting a bullet in the back of your head. Understand?" said the man.

"As always, I understand. Now, where the hell is Cathal?" Jack asked.

The men looked at one another again. This time they smiled.

"He is at the clubhouse," said the man.

Jack felt his legs turn slightly jelly-like as he stood up. He mustered all of his might to give them strength. The gunmen were of the opinion that only a guilty man would have anything to fear. It never seemed to occur to them that even a completely innocent man or women would be scared to death at being placed in such a situation.

The Fair Isle Golf Club on the outskirts of Dundalk was a magnificent building set in almost one hundred acres of the most spectacular countryside. It had only been two short years from the time that Cathal and three other high ranking IRA godfathers stood in the agricultural land with a dream until the day that the President of Ireland cut the ribbon at the opening ceremony. The spectacular speed that every stage of the project had been completed in raised more than a few eyebrows. The planning process in 1970's Ireland was notoriously slow but things could move a little faster with the aid of brown envelopes stuffed with money. The IRA, thanks to a very successful fund raising campaign in America, as well as their criminal activities across the globe, did not lack for cash. The most serious obstacle to the whole process came in the form of Michael Shaw. He was a farmer from the Dundalk area who happened to own ten acres of land right in the middle of the proposed development. Michael was a crafty character and he refused every offer that the developers made. The bigger the offer, the more desperate they appeared, and the stronger became Shaw's bargaining position—or so he thought.

In spite of all their attempts to give the impression of legitimacy, Cathal and his associates were still little more than common gangsters at heart. After several meetings with Shaw, and with a bigger offer on the table each time, Cathal had finally reached the limits of his patience. That night Michael Shaw found himself gagged and bound in the back of a van being driven at high speed towards the southern tip of Ireland. When the van came to a stop Shaw began to cry. He begged for his life. The men who had picked him up and bundled him into the back of the van as he left his local pub said nothing. He was spilled out onto some cold, wet grassland and they drove off. It was several hours before he managed to free himself from the restraints and another three hours before he arrived back home, cold and shaking. The message had been made to him clearly enough and within a few days he had signed over the land and for a price that was much less than the last legitimate offer they had made to him.

As well as providing an acceptable face for the terrorist group, the golf club provided a front to launder money. According to the official financial books the place was bringing in so much alcohol to sell every month that the members of the club would have to be amongst the most rampant drinkers on the whole island of Ireland. No one bothered investigating. It was a very simple scam. The booze was bought legitimately enough. It was supposedly sold to customers for a profit and that's where the criminal money was used. Truth was the club was so exclusive that it had a very low membership and the amount of alcohol being sold simply didn't make sense. As the booze wasn't actually being bought by patrons, it was shipped to the north by fishing boat and sold in small country pubs all across the province—bringing in a tidy sum by way of a bonus.

All this information was imparted to Jack on that first night as he sat in a large bar which was occupied by ten men—six of whom were acting as guards. During his training back in Scotland Jack had been warned never to get drunk. Even a man with cast iron self control was open to saying or doing something stupid when under the influence, but as Jack sat with his new associates he got the feeling that if he didn't match them drink for drink then that really would have been the end of the affair.

The three other men who were drinking with Jack and Cathal were P.J. (Patrick Joseph) Kelly, Callum O'Neil and

Barry Fegan. Kelly was a quiet man. He sat back and sipped on a pint of Guinness all night, observing everything and turning over all that was said with quiet, menacing assurance. O'Neil was full of hot air. He had real pretentions to being the next leader of the movement and he acted more like a politician than a freedom fighter. He assumed that if he was ever to gain enough support for his leadership bid then as many people as possible within the movement would need to know who he was and they would also need to know of the brave acts he was supposed to have carried out. Unfortunately for O'Neil, this was not what the rest of the leadership was looking for in an overall leader. They needed someone who was discrete, someone who could command the loyalty and respect of the men without having to win them over with bullshit. There would soon be a place for men like O'Neil in the newly formed political branch of the movement, but he was never going to lead the Army Council, the body that was in overall command of the group.

Barry Fegan was the man who interested Jack the most. He drank more than the rest of them combined and yet he never once told tales of the missions that he had been on, or the power and wealth that he was in control of. That he was in that group sitting at that table meant that he was very important; that he never let anything slip meant that he would be trusted with some of the IRA's most important secrets. The problem for Jack was how to get him to part with those secrets—alcohol was never going to loosen his lips.

"The wee bastard looked me in the eye and said, you are a dead man, Paddy," O'Neil said, as he explained an encounter with a group of soldiers on the South Armagh border.

"So he squeezes the trigger. Swear to god, I didn't even blink. I just knew that gun was going to jam. I just knew it. So I punched him in the balls, jumped to my feet, took the gun off him and put two bullets in his head. His mates poked their head's out of the armoured car to see what was going on. I fired a short burst at the whore hanging out of the back door. He drops forward. I knew that I didn't have to put myself in danger to get the other fuckers. Three short bursts through the open door and they were dead."

Jack looked confused. O'Neil smiled widely.

"Armoured car? Bullet proof glass?" explained O'Neil. "Come on Martin, think about it. The bullets bounced around on the inside of the car until they hit something soft. Nothing quite as soft as a British soldier."

O'Neil smiled widely. Jack smiled, though he was still none to clear as to what it was that O'Neil found so funny. The alcohol was clearly getting to him.

"That's nothing," Cathal said. "You lads have it easy. You head across the border in the dead of night and do a bit of hunting. Then you head back home, safe in the knowledge that the army can't follow you back into the south. The real heroes are men like Martin. They have to take a shit on their own doorstep. They spend weeks, months or years just waiting for that knock to the door and some big RUC man standing on the other side ready to take you down to Crumlin Road jail to kick seven shades of shite out of you until you tell him what he wants to hear."

The men laughed.

"I don't know," Cathal continued; his tone of voice a little despondent. "It just seems like there is little point to many of these attacks. It hardens public opinion against us but it does nothing to shift public opinion in England towards giving us the north back. We are like a tiny mosquito nipping at the backside of an elephant. We need something big. We need something that will tear the balls off them and get the public on the mainland to rise up and force the government into giving us what we want. We need to show them that they are not safe."

"Another round of pub bombings?" asked O'Neil.

"Nah, that only pissed them off the last time and made them even more determined not to give in," said Cathal.

Cathal took a long sip of his whiskey and a drag of his cigarette before continuing.

"Why do the people on the mainland feel so safe?" he asked.

There was a pause for a moment.

"Because most of our attacks take place in Ireland," suggested O'Neil.

"That's part of it," said Cathal. "But only a small part of it. Let me ask you another question; what does it mean to be English and what would have to happen to take that sense of identity away from them?"

There was another short pause.

"For god's sake men. It wasn't a trick question. What makes the English, English?" Cathal asked again.

"I don't know," said O'Neil. "The Queen? Cricket? Football? Winning two World Wars?"

"Now we are getting somewhere," Cathal said.

O'Neil rolled his eyes and said, "So all we need to do is to beat them at war, on a cricket field, with the Queen watching, and then cut her head off when we are done?"

"If you take the Queen out of the equation and forget about the damn cricket for one minute, you might just be onto something," Cathal said, and then he raised his glass.

For the first time in over an hour, Barry spoke. He had decided that the conversation had gone far enough for the time being. Jack couldn't be sure if Barry didn't want him to hear the rest of the plan, or if he didn't want O'Neil to hear the rest of the plan. Either way, Barry had enough.

"Right gents," Barry said. "We can pick this up again tomorrow."

"Shut up Barry," O'Neil protested. "Let the man have his say. I haven't heard bullshit of this kind of quality for a very long time. Speak on young man; speak on!"

Barry got to his feet. He put his hands on the table and he then leaned in towards O'Neil until their faces were almost touching.

"I said that we can pick this conversation up again in the morning."

There was a tense pause. O'Neil broke the tension of the moment with a laugh.

"For Christ's sake Barry, you really are a tight little fucker. OK, OK we will pick this up again in the morning. Wouldn't want to get on the wrong side of the Gestapo. Man you really are going to have to learn how to relax. You are only a young man and you already look as if you are eighty. If you are finding the pressure of the struggle too much for you then you should let someone know. We have excellent health cover and I'm sure we will be able to get you some help for your poor wee head. There's nothing funny about a gunman in the middle of a nervous breakdown."

O'Neil grinned. Barry did not smile. He continued to hold the pose with his hands on the table until O'Neil got up from his seat and left the room. The normally jolly O'Neil changed his expression as he reached the door and he looked back at Barry. It was an exchange between the two men that told of how one of them was not going to survive if the other man ever held real power within the organisation.

The complex had its own luxury hotel attached and Jack was escorted to a suite that overlooked the course. That room was to be his base of operations for the duration of his stay with the gunmen. That they were keeping him so close to the centre of their power meant one of two things—they either trusted him completely, or, they didn't trust him at all and they wanted to keep an eye on him at all times. Jack favoured the second of those two options.

In the days that followed Jack was kept at a safe distance whenever meetings were taking place. There was a constant stream of new faces coming and going. Cathal's grand plan would be revealed to him only if they thought that he needed to know, and for the time being, he did not need to know. From the comfort of his room he watched as various groups of men arrived at the complex before being escorted onto the greens for a game and a chat with one of the top brass. Jack was not a prisoner in those early days as he was free to come and go as he pleased, and he could use any of the facilities to keep himself entertained. He was just kept out of the loop as no one told him anything about the nature of the many meetings that were taking place on the greens and in the bar. Even Cathal had gone dark on him. There were no more late night, indiscrete, drinking sessions.

As the days rolled into weeks Jack couldn't help but feel that in spite of all the luxury surrounding him, and the absence of bars on the windows, the complex was beginning to resemble a prison. On the Monday of the third week Jack got an early morning call. It was Barry.

"You and me are heading to Dublin on a bit of business," Barry said. "I'll meet you out the front in ten minutes."

Jack hadn't time to say a word before Barry closed the door to Jack's room and he left. As Jack had no idea where they were going or what kind of business they were to conduct, he had no idea what he should wear. If it was the kind of business that went on at the golf club then a suit would have been in order. If it was the kind of business carried out in an empty farmhouse in deepest, darkest Sligo, then a pair of jeans and a dark pullover would have been more appropriate. During the few weeks that he had been at the complex he had been brought several outfits to wear. They had even bought him a television and a radio for his room.

The more that he thought about it the more likely it was that the business Barry had in mind was not going to require a suit. Barry looked like an enforcer and had their mission been legitimate business, then surely it would have been carried out at the complex. Jeans and a jumper it was.

Barry was waiting for Jack as promised. He was in a lime green BMW. Jack liked the style of the car but the colour left a lot to be desired. Barry was wearing jeans and a leather jacket even though the temperature that morning was already verging on the hot. Barry was characteristically quiet and Jack endorsed himself to his sensibilities but keeping quiet. Jack knew that there was little point in asking Barry about what they were doing or even where they were going as Barry would have told him already if he thought that he needed to know. Some of the others used secrecy as some kind of power trip—they knew things that he didn't and that's why they were much more important than him—but Barry used silence as a survival technique.

An hour out of Dundalk and the two men had not exchanged a single word. Jack tried to look as calm as possible about the situation but the longer the journey lasted the more obsessed he became with studying road signs and checking his mirror for any indication that they were being followed. They pulled onto the ring road around Dublin. Jack assumed that by using the road which mainly bypassed the city that they were ultimately heading further south. His deduction fell by the wayside when they pulled into an estate made up of council flats in the north of the city. Barry brought the car to a stop in the middle of the large courtyard that served as a car park and play ground; a rallying point for rioters and a place where criminal commerce was conducted in the open—prostitution, drugs, stolen goods, counterfeit goods—it was a criminal market place that went largely undisturbed by the local police. The Irish police were a small, poorly equipped force and a huge part of their budget was set aside to fight Republican terrorists. Partly the anti-terror money was there to appease the British state. The British had made several thinly veiled threats over the years to send troops across the border to "assist" the Irish government with their attempt to round up the IRA—especially in the aftermath of a spectacular atrocity. The other part of the anti-terror money was there quite legitimately—the IRA's ultimate goal was to establish a socialist Irish Republic. Such a state would have no place for the men who currently ran the country. The government had to play a very clever game.

It was a very fragile balancing act. Many people in the Irish Republic were entirely behind the ultimate aims of the IRA even if they did not agree with all of the methods that they employed to reach that objective. If the government cracked down too heavily on the IRA then they risked suffering the wrath of the people; if they did nothing to curtail the terror group then they faced self annihilation, either at the hands of the IRA, or at the hands of the British state.

Ghettoes such as the one that Barry and Jack had just entered were strong IRA recruiting grounds. The people were poor and they often considered themselves to be largely forgotten by the rest of the country. The new socialist state that the prophets from the IRA spoke of in the pubs and clubs around Dublin held huge appeal for them. The people of those estates rallied behind some of the most ruthless gangsters ever to have graced the back streets of any world city. They were kings in their own right and they made life and death decisions on a whim. Men and boys were dragged from their beds in the middle of the night, tortured and then executed, on the basis on little more than hearsay. They sent gangs of young men and women out into the more affluent parts of the city to carry out robberies, all in the name of some glorious future that was never going to materialise. The godfathers grew richer and men like Barry moved away from the filth and squalor of their city strongholds. But they were never completely free from them.

Barry stopped the car's engine and he casually lit up a cigarette. They waited. After five minutes two teenage boys walked past their car. One of the boys looked around. He stopped for a moment when he saw Barry. The lads ran off into one of the blocks. A couple of minutes after the boys went inside a man in his mid-twenties and a teenage girl came out. The man kissed the girl and then she walked away. He came over to their car and he got into the back seat.

"Jesus, Barry," the young man began. "I wish you would tell me when you are coming down."

"Why Paddy? So you can hide the drugs and whores and then tell me that business is slow?" Barry said, with no emotion in his voice or on his face.

"Jesus, Barry, if you can get more out of these bastards then be my guest. Times have been tough all over. For most of us anyway. Nice car by the way. Will she take us faster to a united Ireland?" Paddy quipped.

Barry didn't react.

"Give me this month's total," Barry said.

Paddy pulled an envelope out from inside his jacket and handed it to Barry.

"There's 20K in there. Not bad considering all that has been going on. The Guarda have been right up my arsehole since those bastards starting blowing up women and children on the mainland," Paddy complained.

"My heart bleeds for you. I put you in charge of Dublin because you know how to get blood out of stones. If you'd spend less time banging whores and more time keeping an eye on your turf, then maybe you could hand over the kind of money you should be handing over."

"Fuck off Barry. You have no idea what it's like down here in the real world," Paddy said.

For a moment there was nothing more said.

"So, who's your wee friend?" Paddy asked.

"He's your replacement if you don't get your act together," snarled Barry.

"Jesus, Barry, message received. You can be a complete prick at times," Paddy protested.

"I'm serious," Barry said. "If you can't sort your act out by next month then I will put someone else in charge. I don't have to tell you just how shit the pension plan is."

"OK, OK. Fuck's sake. You are worse than my Ma when you start going on about something. But if you want to see the numbers go up you will have to send me some more men. As the money has gone down the drugs market has gone up. You know? People trying to find a way to forget just how

eir lives are? We have not been quick enough to tap
ırket and one or two entrepreneurs have stepped in
to fill the gap. The brother of that cunt you just saw leaving
was one of them. Couple of vodkas and a good hard ride and
she'd tell me anything."

"That's good. Maybe she can tell you where her brother
is going to be tonight. Maybe, if it's not too much trouble,
you can take a few of the fifty men that you already have at
your disposal and teach him a lesson? Just make sure that
you put out the word that he was a drugs dealer and that he
had been warned several times to stop selling poison to the
children of Dublin. The IRA is against drugs. At least until
we can get a reliable supply in place," Barry added, smiling
momentarily.

"Yeah, she knows I'm up to my nuts in drugs. She knows
that I am in the IRA. She is a mouthy wee bitch and when
we crucify her brother she will be on the radio and television
giving it what for."

Barry started the engine of the car. That was the signal to
Paddy that the conversation was at an end. Paddy opened
the door.

"What should I do about the girl?" he asked.

"I don't care and I don't want to know. All I can tell you
for sure is that if she starts shooting her mouth off to the
press, it will be you who will take the fall."

"That's a damn shame," Paddy said, with a faraway look
on his face. "She was a real good ride."

He got out of the car. Barry and Jack drove off. For a short
time there was nothing more said. Then, out of the blue,
Barry stared to talk.

"I grew up in this shit hole," he said. "It used to be bearable
but in the last ten years it has turned into a real swamp. The
dregs from all over Ireland are dumped here. The Guarda
keep them contained for the most part, but the estates are
growing larger year by year. There is nothing else for them
to do other than get high, get drunk, screw and have kids.

Still, they hand over a nice little bundle of pocket money for me every month and when we are looking for some dumbass to carry out a risky shooting or bombing, this is definitely the place to shop. The less they have, the easier they are to control."

"It can't be easy for them," Jack said, trying to be respectful of the fact that this was where Barry was from.

"Fuck them. No one is stopping them from getting up off their arses and making something of their lives. If they are happy to live in their own shit then there is no point complaining to the rest of us," Barry added, with a real vein of bitterness and disgust running through his words.

"This is where I made my start," Barry continued. "I gave Paddy the same opportunity that I was given. What the dumb fuck doesn't know is that I was very good friends with his Ma back in the day. I mean, I was really good friends. When I say that I see something of myself in the lad, there is more truth in that than I'd ever admit to anyone, least of all him."

Jack smiled.

"Son or no son, if he doesn't soon pull his head out of his arse then he is going to find himself having a very stormy conversation with a baseball bat. We might leave the nails out of the end of it. After all, blood is thicker than water."

Barry smiled again. It was a fleeting smile as if somewhere in his DNA the genes for joy had been reprogrammed. Joy was a weakness and Barry was not weak.

"So Martin, are there any wee ones in your life?" Barry asked.

"Nah, I never felt the need."

"Christ almighty. And you call yourself a good catholic boy?"

Jack smiled.

"No family at all then?" quizzed Barry.

"Nope. There is just me."

"Pity. Family is so important. I have six kids with my wife. Three more that she knows fuck all about. If she ever did find out about them, you can be damn sure that I wouldn't be having any more kids with any woman."

Jack smiled again. It was so hard to get a read on Barry. Jack didn't want to smile too much in case he thought that he was in some way trying to play him; but at the same time he didn't want to ignore his attempts at humour in case that offended him. It was a very hard balance to reach.

"We have been looking into you for a long time, Martin," Barry said. "You have impressed us a great deal. We have been planning an operation that needs ten or so good men. Men we can trust. Men like you."

"Men with no families," Jack said.

He knew that if he didn't show some hesitation to what he was being told, Barry might get suspicious.

There was a pause.

"Now that you mention it, there is a higher than usual chance that some of you won't come back. Men with no family ties was a factor in the selection process. But it is not the most important factor. Your accent is more important than your lack of a family."

Jack said nothing.

"You will need to receive several weeks of intensive training. We will also need to practice the attack several times. You know, the normal sort of bullshit? Martin, this is the big one. This is the attack in this war that will either bring us a united Ireland or it will bring the full weight of the British military state down on this entire island."

When the moment had finally arrived—the one that he had been working towards for so many years—he was impassive. He should have been feeling joy; he should have been feeling worried; he should have been feeling something. There was nothing.

"I am going to take you to meet the other members of your team," Barry explained. "They are all long standing volunteers. Like yourself, they have all been out on missions and most importantly—they have all come back from those missions safe and well. You will be surrounded and supported by the best of the best. No pressure, but this is the single most important mission that the IRA has carried out in its entire history."

"No pressure then," Jack said, with a grin.

They drove through the busy city streets and eventually they pulled into a modern housing estate in a better part of town. Barry swung the car into the driveway of one of the houses, stopping inches from a brown Ford Escort. They got out and walked up to the front of the house. Barry rang the bell and within moments a blond haired man in his mid-twenties opened the front door to them. Barry went to go inside the house but the man put out a hand to stop him.

"Wipe your feet. I've just put down new carpet," said the man.

Barry wiped his feet for a sarcastically long time on the brown, coconut coir mat. The man took his hand away from Barry and he went inside. Jack followed him. The man pushed past Barry and led them through to the living room. Two men were sitting in the living room drinking tea and eating chocolate digestives. It was a scene of utter civility and nothing like the boastful, drunken, swearing affairs that Jack had come to expect.

"Gentlemen," Barry began. "This is Martin. He's the last member of your team. Martin, sitting on the left is John, and the ugly bastard sitting on the right is Fat John. The queer housewife who let us in is Gerald. Though do feel free to call him Doris. Normal rules apply. Fat John is leading the group. Gerald is armoury officer. John is in charge of transport and Martin is our fixer. He's going to get us access to the targets. Remember, first names only. No small talk. You will spend many long nights together in the coming weeks but no matter how much you are tempted, you say nothing to any other member of the group that could be used to identify you. Common sense stuff lads, that's all."

They looked each other up and down and nodded their

heads to indicate that they understood and agreed to the terms that Barry was setting out for them.

"I'll keep the bullshit to a minimum. You know how important all of you are to the movement. You all know how important this mission is to a united Ireland. You all know this already and you don't need me to stand here and tell you that all over again," Barry began. "I'll get right to the point. This is going to be our most devastating attack. This is going to be the single battle in this war that will send the Brits home. The mission will take place in the north. We had thought about carrying it out on the mainland but there is too much risk that it could backfire if we do. We are going to drive four of the biggest bombs that we have ever assembled into the heart of a town in the north on a busy Saturday morning and then set them off simultaneously. This attack will leave hundreds dead. I'm talking men, women and children. I'm talking about pregnant women. I'm talking about pictures on the news of parts of children being brushed up off the road and shovelled into plastic bin bags. In short; I'm talking about an almost inhuman act. I tell you this not to impress you. I tell you this so that if you have any doubts, or think that you might develop any doubts, now is the time to walk away. In a few minutes I will give you details about the attack, including the target itself and after that you will not be able to say no. Well you can say no, but it will be the last no that will ever pass your lips. Except for the 'no don't put that gun to my head'. Or, 'no, don't pull the trigger.' All bullshit aside. I will ask you all one last time if you have any doubts. Last chance to walk away from this."

He turned to Fat John. Fat John nodded yes. He turned to John. John nodded yes. He turned to Gerald. Gerald nodded yes. He turned to Jack. There was a dramatic pause. Jack nodded yes.

14

The Gates of Hell

The normally straightforward Barry milked the moment for every drop of drama as the men stood in silence and looked at one another. As far as Jack was concerned, they had never met before, complete strangers who were getting together for the first time to discuss an act of such utter barbarity that it would be carried by news services all around the world. Jack knew what his role in the scheme really was—to put a stop to it—but the pragmatic part of his mind thought that the attack would probably do more damage to the IRA if it went ahead. It might even force them into calling an end to their war once and for all. Their main source of funding came from the US and in the light of a number of terrorist attacks against US airliners there was a real ground swell of public opinion forming against all terror groups. The Irish had always been a special case. They were not foreign speaking strangers with a blind hatred for the American way of life. To many Americans, especially those with Irish ancestry, the IRA were brave freedom fighters. The conflict was regarded as a romantic fight between a small number of good men against the full might of an evil British Empire. The planned attack in Lisburn would change that perception forever. There was nothing brave about killing woman and children in cold blood and it would be a brave fund raiser who would hold out a collection tin in a Boston bar in support of baby killers.

Jack shook the thought. It was something that he could never let happen; not even if the sacrifice on that day would stop others from dying in the future. Another thought hit him and it left him feeling cold. If he was having that thought then he could be certain that one of the strategic planners back in London would also have that thought. With images of bombed out, blood splattered pubs across England still fresh in the minds of many, was it such a stretch that they would allow Lisburn to go ahead? It was a dirty war and the normal rules and civility of war were completely absent. Both sides were capable of just about anything. He set that discussion to one said and focused his attention on Barry, who had just returned to the room after going outside to his car. He had a large blue and grey holdall with him which he set on the floor next to a coffee table. He unzipped the bag, removed a handful of papers and began to arrange them on the table. Instinctively the men gathered around the table.

Barry cleared his throat.

"OK lads," Barry began. "This is a just a brief run through for what we have planned. As we get closer to the target date we may need to make a few alterations but for the most part this is the plan. We selected the target for a number of reasons. The main reason is that it contains one of the largest army bases in the whole of the occupied six counties."

Barry pointed at a red X on the page.

"The victims of the attack will include off duty soldiers; their wives and children. The rest of the town is mainly made up of businesses that serve the base. I don't need to tell you what football teams those bastards cheer for. They have been very good at keeping Catholics from owning shops and other businesses in the town, and any time a house goes on the market they would rather sell it to a Protestant than a Catholic, even if that means losing money. Bottom line; we can do some serious damage and be reasonably sure that very few from our own side will get caught up in the explosions. If we tried this in the centre of Belfast we would have no way of knowing who would be there, or what foot they kicked with.

"The next main reason that we went for Lisburn is access. There is no real way to know how the security forces will respond on the day of the attack. They will start to close roads around the town but because of the high casualty rates and range of the attacks they will be stretched pretty thin. They simply will not have the manpower to close every route out of town. There should be no problem making your escape. If you can't get onto the main dual-carriageway heading south directly, you will have loads of alternative roads that you can use to join it. There are three or four at Banbridge and half dozen at Newry. It might even be an idea to head to somewhere out of the way like Newcastle in the Mournes. You know? You keep your options open and use the path of least resistance on the day. Commonsense stuff.

"The attack itself it pretty simple. We are going to use several large vehicles and a number of small car bombs. The car bombs are going to go off half an hour before the Lisburn attack all over Belfast. Lisburn is only six miles from Belfast and by the time we are ready to stage the main attacks in Lisburn there should be quite a lot of the army tied up with the bombs in Belfast. There are over three thousand soldiers at the Lisburn base. Fortunately for us there is only one entrance. Those who are not responding to the bombs in Belfast will be contained. A couple of local lads are going to hijack two lorries and then abandon them in the middle of the road, north and south of the entrance. A few wires and some other bullshit inside the lorries with keep the army in the base until they have time to have them properly investigated. That being said, once the main bombs go off they will find a way to get out of the base; even if that means knocking down part of the security wall so that they are clear of the lorries. It will be their wives and children who are caught up in the attack and no wall is going to keep them back. The emotional chaos will also help you get away. These men will not be thinking clearly as they search through the rubble for their loved ones. It is not a pleasant thought, but this has been a long and unpleasant war. If you need me to explain why this is morally justified then you ought not to be a volunteer in the IRA. Simple as that."

Jack knew exactly what he was referring to. In his time in Ireland, living in the Republican community, he had listened to many tales of woe. Discrimination and even murder against the Catholic population by a tyrannical Protestant ruling class. The tales were horrific and the Republican response heroic. Families driven from their homes; discrimination in the workplace; political intimidation; harassment from a police force that is largely comprised of members from the Protestant community. It was a long list. It was a terrible list. It was a list that was to very effectively draw in new recruits and stir to action active members. Theirs was a just war. The only problem was the Protestants had their own list that was every bit as long and every bit as disturbing. Jack's mother reminded him often that there were three sides to every story; one side of the story, the other side of the story and the real story. That real story had got lost somewhere in the mucky mists of Irish history and it was gone forever.

"Everything I have mentioned so far is simply setting the stage for the main event. And that is where you lads come in. The centre of the town is a pedestrian zone. The only vehicles that can enter that zone unopposed are security vehicles, council vehicles and delivery vans and lorries. Shop owners can temporarily bring their own vans and cars into the zone, but they must display a permit. What we have planned is going to require something the size of a lorry or a van. Ideally lorries would be my choice but the surveillance that we have carried out in the area shows that it is very unlikely that four lorries would be in the area on a Saturday at one time. Most of the businesses take deliveries on Mondays and Thursdays. We reckon that the least suspicious set up would be one bread lorry; two road sweepers and a lorry delivering beer. We would normally hijack a vehicle the day before the attack, then load the weapon and drive it to the target.

Lisburn council have very distinctive dark blue vehicles and if we steal two of them the day before you can be sure the police will be looking out for them. It is too risky. We have bought two surplus street sweepers from Newry and Mourne council and we are in the process of having them re-sprayed and kitted out to look like Lisburn council sweepers. The lorries will be made up to look like they belong to local companies. Everything to keep a low profile. This operation has been in the planning for well over a year and if we are successful it will mark a day that no one on this island, or on mainland GB will ever forget."

Fat John interrupted.

"You say we bought them? Surely that is going to leave a paper trail? How are we going to explain that after the attack?" he asked.

"The paper trail will lead nowhere," Barry explained. "Well, that's not strictly true. The paper trail will lead to people who never existed, or people who are long since dead."

Barry grinned, "It used to be said that the only way out of the IRA was death; that's not the case anymore. We are stealing their identities, for a little while. To be honest, that was the one thing that worried me. That some sharp-eyed little shit in an office somewhere spots something out of the ordinary. No need to worry. We have two supporters working in the Vehicle Licensing Office in Colerain. We slipped them a few pounds—job done."

Jack couldn't believe Barry's confidence in the plan. If the devastation was as comprehensive as he maintained then there would be no stone that was left unturned. The men working in the Vehicle Licensing Office would be interrogated to the nth degree, using means that no civilised nation would ever consider using.

Barry turned to the map again. He pointed to the map as he spoke. His finger moved swiftly across the paper and there was not a single trace of nervousness or apprehension.

This plan was his obsession and he could replay it with his eyes closed.

"The first two devices will explode at the same time. They will be here and here. Right in the middle of the main shopping area. Those who aren't killed in the first two blasts will be escorted towards the end of this street, at both ends, depending on where they are when the bombs go off. Five minutes after the first two blasts, the second and third bombs will explode—simultaneously. One at each end of the street. That should take care of most of the survivors, as well as any police or army who have made it to the area to help."

A chill ran through Jack's body as Barry described mass murder with such calculating clam. In that instant another heart stopping thought struck him—with such fanatical devotion and ruthless abandon, these men might actually win the war.

"The bombs will be on timers," Barry continued. "This will give you some time to make your escape, but only a little time. If we put the vehicles in place too soon then there is a risk that someone will notice them and call the security forces. The maximum time that you have between leaving the device and getting away will be thirty minutes. Any longer than that and we risk blowing the entire operation. That doesn't give you a lot of time to be well on your way to the border, but with the other diversions already in place, you should not need any more time than that."

There was a pause as Barry let the men digest what was being asked of them. Three of them were weighing up the morality of what was being asked of them, as well as the personal risk that they were going to subjected to. Jack had his mind in top gear working on how he was going to stop the slaughter and walk away from it alive. They were a tense few moments.

"So lads; what do you think?" Barry asked.

"I think it is madness. I think your head is cut," said John. "I think that it has to be the craziest plan I have ever heard. I love it."

He smiled. Barry returned with a fleeting smile of his own.

The others simply nodded their heads to indicate that they too agreed with what they were being asked to do.

"Men, I know what is being asked of you," Barry said. "I know that when those bombs go off and those people die, none of you will ever be the same again. No one on this island will ever be the same again. You will be reviled and hated by everyone. And I mean everyone. There will be a queue of people from your own side just lining up to condemn you and this time they will mean every word of it. The Americans will turn on us. The church will turn on us. Every wee lad in a Republican area who only ever wanted to grow up to join the IRA, will turn on us. In the months and years that will follow we will be the most hated people on the face of this planet. The Brits will round us up in the thousands and throw us in prison without a trial. Hell, they will throw anyone you have ever talked to in prison. They will harass our wives and children. Old people will be pulled from their beds in the middle of the night to be searched and interrogated. But it will all be worth it. The Brits will turn in on themselves. Every town and city in England will go into lockdown. In their attempt to protect themselves they will destroy their society. It will only be a matter of time before the people living in those towns and cities will demand that they have their old way of life back. There is only one way that any British government can achieve that—by giving us what they want. Even then, they will not simply hand over the keys to the north to the IRA. Power will be given to moderate politicians from Dublin. But they will be our politicians. They will be Irishmen."

The disgust and horror that Jack felt about what was being discussed would never go away, but as he listened to Barry give his speech he understood a little about why so many young men and women were drawn into their war. It was powerful stuff, if morally bankrupt and inhuman. Jack nodded his head in all the right places as Barry continued to spew his half-baked patriotism. The rant lasted another ten minutes, with Barry speaking more like a preacher out to convert the unenlightened rather than someone who was already speaking to the converted. It was only when Barry noticed that the head nodding had stopped and his audience was now shuffling uncomfortably in their seats, with a fixed gaze of apathy on their faces that he finally relented. He cleared his throat and changed tone from that of wide-eyed dreamer to hardened commander who would never take no for an answer.

"There is a lot that needs to be put in place before we can execute this operation. As with all operations the field units have been left in the dark until the end of the process before being informed. One leak anywhere and we will all go down for life. It only takes one drunken boast in a pub to bring the British army raining down us like the unholy fires of hell. From this point on none of you will have any contact with the outside world. Those of you who have not said goodbye to your wives and children will not get the chance to do so in person, but a messenger will be sent to them to pass along whatever you need to say. This will be done verbally. I know that it is far from ideal but I am afraid the security implications of direct contact with your family are simply too much."

"Not over stating our importance here," John began, "but surely we are being watched on and off by the security forces? Do you not think that they will find it a bit odd if we simply disappear off the face of the earth?"

"We have thought of that too," Barry explained. "We will leak information about a group of volunteers making a trip to South America to buy weapons. As we approach the date of the attack we will leak the names of those volunteers. The Brits or the Irish forces will not be looking for you if they think that you are walking around Colombia with a shopping cart looking for AK-47's. By the time the British have the claims investigated by their agents in that part of the world, it will be much too late for them to piece the operation together, much less do anything about it."

The men looked at each other again. For Jack this was his first time attending a meeting where an upcoming major operation was discussed, but for the others, they had been down this road many times—or so Jack assumed. The looks on their faces betrayed many of their thoughts; from uncertainty and fear, to enthusiasm and an almost disturbing sense of being impressed. If these men were impressed by this plan then there really was something to be impressed about.

"When we leave Dublin we will head back up the coast road to Dundalk and we will make camp at the course. There will be one or two field trips and you will receive some intensive training from the very best that this organisation has to offer."

Jack stood on a smile as he imagined Barry as a US drill sergeant on the parade grounds addressing a bunch of raw recruits.

"When we get back to base I will introduce you to our lucky charm," Barry said to Jack as they left the house. He then grinned. It may not have been the largest smile Jack had ever witnessed, but it was genuine.

15

The "Lucky Charm"

They drove in a three vehicle convoy back to the golf course. Jack said very little on the journey back north except for a few comments about the countryside or the monuments that they passed. He was taken by the number of reminders of British rule in Ireland that were littered all over the Irish countryside—from statues of the long gone aristocracy to the distinctively shaped Royal Mail post boxes—now painted green, but still bearing the Royal insignia. These reminders of the past gave Jack some insight into why men like Barry still clung onto historical grievances—it was history, but it was only just history, and for many men and women still alive at that time it all happened in their lifetime.

Much of the tension that Barry had carried on the way down to Dublin had now gone and even though the topic of conversation never drifted towards the operation, he was still in a very chatty mood. He was an encyclopaedia of historical knowledge and there wasn't a town or village that they passed through where Barry didn't have some story to accompany it. Fairly anonymous looking fields were the scenes for this battle or that massacre. The stories were rich in detail and told with great skill but as none of them happened in the recent past they were no more than stories. Jack wondered if this was because the "great battles" of the recent decades were dirty and sneaky and fought with a sense of shame that would have left the brave men and women whose deaths carved out the nation of Ireland spinning in their graves.

It was dusk by they time got back to his room. He was exhausted. The trip hadn't taken long but the psychological aspects accompanying what he had been told and what he still needed to do were draining. He removed his jacket and threw it on the floor before falling back onto the bed. Within minutes he was sleeping. He had told Barry that he didn't want anything to eat until later and he hoped that request would afford him a few hours of rest. It was an inaccessible hope.

Half an hour into his doze and Jack woke up. At first he thought he was still dreaming but it soon became clear that nothing could be farther from the truth. Standing by the side of his bed, in full vestments, was a priest. The holy man gave Jack the sign of the cross.

"Father?" Jack said, in a low, confused voice.

"I am here to read you the last rights," said the priest.

The priest's words did nothing to dispel Jack's confusion.

"Last rights?"

The priest began to mumble something. Jack looked at him with grave concern. Why was he there? Did all volunteers get to meet with a priest before they went out on a dangerous mission? Had they finally realised that he was a spy and this was the night when he would make that final car journey into the ever after? There was an explosion of laughter from the other side of the room. Jack turned around to find Barry bent double through laughing. It took Barry a few minutes to regain his composure. When he did, he quickly moved across to the priest and he put his arm around him.

"This is Father Owen. He's a real life, honest to god priest, who has more than a passing interest in our cause. In Republican circles he is an absolute legend. He really is here to give you the last rights," explained Barry.

His worth to the Republican movement was of some interest to Jack. He often wondered how they could carry out the atrocities given how anti-Christian such actions were. Surely there would be no father confessor willing to offer them absolution?

However, what was of greater interest to him at that moment was why the priest was in his room offering to give him the last rights. A terrible thought struck him at that moment—after all the careful preparation and planning, after all the boring history lessons back in London, no one had ever stopped to tell him what the last rights actually were. If there was some part of the proceedings that required him to say or do something, then he was screwed—he simply had no idea. His mind frantically searched for an answer. Surely it must have been documented in a book that he read, or a film or TV show that he had watched. There was nothing that hit him no matter how hard he searched the archives of his brain.

Improvising, Jack jumped up off the bed and he looked the priest right in the eye. The priest didn't flinch. He had known hard men like Jack all his life and he had always stood his ground in a confrontation.

"If you don't mind Father," Jack said. "Since the death of my mother, God and I haven't been all that close."

Barry slapped Jack on the arm.

"For Christ's sake Jack, we were only messing with your head. You will have to learn how to lighten up or the stress will kill you," Barry said.

"Either the stress, or a one thousand pound bomb going off prematurely in the lorry that you are driving," said the priest, without a trace of irony.

Jack looked at Barry with surprise. Why would this man be told what was about to happen? What happened to all the bullshit about mission security? Were they going to hold the priest at the golf course until after the attack? It made little sense to Jack.

"We will see you in the bar in five minutes," Barry said, before he and the priest left Jack's room.

As was normal whenever official IRA business was being conducted, the bar was devoid of members of the general public. Barry and the priest were standing by the bar as Jack approached them. The sound of Jack's shoes on the wooden floor was enough to grab their attention and both men turned to face him in a synchronised motion. They were standing next to two stools.

"Martin," Barry beamed. He patted the seat of one of the stools. "We thought you might need to sit down following your wee scare?"

"Funny man, Barry," Jack said before sitting on a stool next to Barry. The other two men sat down too.

"This is Father Joseph Channey. The lucky charm," Barry said.

Jack extended a hand and the priest took it.

"Very pleased to meet you Father. Properly."

"The pleasure is all mine," said the priest.

Jack weighed up this new player in the drama and the impression being formed in his mind was somewhat at odds with the reality of the situation. With his dark hair and good looks, this guy looked more like a movie star than he did a priest. Jack would not have been surprised to see a man such as this driving around the Irish countryside with a dolly bird sitting next to him.

Jack didn't need to order a drink as a whiskey over ice was already waiting for him on the bar. Jack lifted the glass and he took a long sip before putting it back down and addressing Father Channey directly.

"As neither of you are going to tell me; why lucky charm?"

The priest grinned.

"Let me tell you a little story," Barry interrupted.

Jack was getting more than a little tired of Barry and his little stories. Jack missed the strong, silent Barry, who could kill you with a simple stare.

"This is the only one in the history of the Republican movement to single handedly take on the British army, the RUC and a load of sympathisers all at one time, and then walk away. Not only did he walk away, but he got caught first and the Brits had all the evidence that they needed to lock him away for life. The Church knew what he had done as well and how did they punish him? They only bloody moved him to a better parish and gave him a pay raise. Talk about a jammy bastard."

Jack looked at Barry as if he had gone mad.

"I swear to god," Barry said, flinging his hands up. "Every last word of it is true. He planted three bombs in a wee village in Tyrone back in '72. Took out three SS RUC, four soldiers and three touts. All without breaking a sweat. The man is a legend. Joe planted the bombs in broad daylight in front of dozens of witnesses. No one at the time thought to ask him what he was doing. He met a police patrol while he was still carrying one of the bombs in a holdall. Calm as you like Joe puts the holdall down on the ground and he talks to the officers for a few minutes about football. Then he was on his way. It was one of those pigs who recognised part of the holdall after the forensic investigation."

"So why wasn't he convicted?" asked Jacked.

Barry smiled again.

"Convicted? He wasn't even arrested," Barry said. "The local RUC lads were just about to head out to make the arrest after evening Mass. They got a phone call from someone at the Northern Ireland Office to hold off. Next thing they knew they were being surrounded by the top brass from the security services telling them that all information related to their investigation of Joe was to be buried. The Bishop moved him from the north to a picturesque wee parish across the border. He was told never to do anything like that again, and look at his wee face; doesn't he look just like the kind of man who would keep his promise?"

"What the hell were you holding over them?" Jack asked, to Joe.

"Only this," Joe replied, tugging on his collar.

"He killed ten people, they caught him red-handed and they let him go just because he was a priest?"

Jack couldn't hide his disbelief.

"The Lord really does work in very mysterious ways," Barry smirked.

"That is bullshit," Jack said. "There is no way they would simply let them him get away with murder like that. No way."

Barry leaned in towards Jack.

"As true as I am sitting here. They let him away with it. The church and the government got together and they decided that if it ever got out that a Catholic priest was in the IRA, never mind involved in murders, then the country would have slid into civil war. The Prods would have burned down churches and priests' houses all over the north. Our side would have risen up to defend such a direct attack on the heart of their religion. It would have been anarchy."

Barry leaned back. Jack couldn't believe what he was hearing. Although Barry was very straightforward in what he normally said and what he did, there was simply no way that such a conspiracy would ever have remained hidden. One of the police officers who were going to arrest Joe would have said something. It simply could not have happened.

"Whenever we are heading out on a big operation we always call in Father Joe to say a wee prayer and bring us luck," Barry added.

Jack raised his glass to the priest.

"I'll take your good luck at any rate," Jack said.

The three men talked and drank into the small hours of the morning. Joe told his story in his own words. There was something very chilling about listening to a man of God as he calmly recalled the calculating way in which he brought the lives of ten people to an end. He showed regret, and it was a very hard extracted regret, for the death of a ten year old boy caught up in one of the blasts. The boy had been a member of Joe's own parish. He knew the lad from the time that he was a baby. Barry felt no such remorse for the child's death. The boy's father ran the local petrol station and it was a well known fact that he served fuel to members of the police—even something so simple was viewed as a treasonous act in the eyes of some volunteers. Father Joe did not accept guilt by association, or birth, as any reason why someone should die. Jack smiled warily—another cold blooded serial killer with a set of morals that made a mockery of morality itself—just what Ireland needed.

As Jack fell onto his bed in the early hours of the morning, and with his head spinning, he was convinced that Joe was telling the truth. He would check the story out when he next went back to London. Lucky charms do come in some strange and unusual shapes and sizes, Jack mused as he drifted off to sleep.

16

Time Flies...

Tax return day. Dentist appointment. Hospital operation. There were some events that to Jack seemed to alter the very fabric of time itself. If it was something that he was dreading or something that was going to bore him, time leading up to the event would always speed up. Conversely, if the event, such as Christmas or a family holiday, was something that he was looking forward to then he could be sure that the days leading up to it would slow down to a painful crawl. Time was a fickle bitch and she teased Jack relentlessly.

Although he had no idea when the attack was going to take place he got the feeling that it was sometime soon and that made each and every day run along a little bit more slowly. Barry had promised that they would be intensively trained by the very best that the IRA had to offer, but so far Jack saw very little by way of specialised training. He had naturally assumed that there would be a certain amount of instruction on how to assemble and disassemble their bombs, should it come to that. There was nothing. That worried jack. He needed to know how to deactivate the device and so he raised the issue when he was out for a walk on the greens one morning with Barry.

"What do we do if it all goes tits up?" Jack asked.

"You get the hell out of there as fast as you can, is what you do. But remember the area will be crawling with police and army. If you do go on the run you will be completely on your own and I really don't fancy your chances. Just don't take any stupid risks. They will barely need an excuse to shoot you on the spot and if you give them that excuse, you don't stand a chance. Play it smart. If you are alive and in prison then there is a chance that one day you will be free. Dead in a field and you are no good to me."

"Sure Barry, I understand all that, but what I mean is how do I check that the bomb is correctly set?"

"That will all be done for you. You don't need to worry about it at all."

"I can't help worrying about it," Jack said forcefully. "I don't know. What if something happens? Something as simple as the lorry hitting a big pothole. If I pull over and check the bomb; how can I be sure that it is still working? I wouldn't have the first idea what I would be looking for."

"And you won't need to know. Like I said, we have all of this covered. You will have an explosives expert travelling with you on the day of the attack. They will be able to deal with any problems that may arise."

Given the number of devices involved and the number of men in their team, Jack had assumed that they would be travelling on their own to Lisburn. In fact, his plan to stop the attack and alert the authorities depended on it. The revelation threw a mighty spanner in the works. Everything would have to be re-worked.

"Anything else?" Barry asked.

"Will I be armed?" Jack asked.

"It is probably best that you aren't. If you get stopped by a security patrol they will be much more interested in searching you than they will be in searching your lorry."

Jack paused as he gave Barry time to notice the look of disappointment he was wearing.

"Something wrong?" Barry asked.

"Not really. I would just prefer to have a weapon with me, that's all. I know that if it came to a shoot-out with the army or several policemen, it would be madness to even try. But what if it is only one soldier or one RUC man standing between me and freedom? I would feel like an idiot."

Barry grinned widely.

"Christ, you really are a wee worrier. If it makes you feel any better I will sort you out with a gun. I will see if we can fix you up with air support and a couple of tanks while I'm at it."

Jack smiled, but not at Barry's humour—the gun would take care of the explosives expert—his plan was back on track.

"Thanks Barry," Jack said.

After ten days of intensive training Jack felt that he knew all that there was to know about driving a lorry. The driving lessons made up the vast majority of what they received by way of instructions but there were a couple of training sessions that rivalled what he had been shown when he first joined the service—again highlighting just how well organised and dangerous this group was.

The most important of those training exercises, according to Barry, was on how to evade capture. This included tips on camouflage and how to hide their scent so that dogs could not be used to track them. They were also shown how to hotwire various vehicles as well as how to make improvised explosive devices out of household chemicals.

The second lesson was on how to spot sympathisers in any town and village between Lisburn and the relative safety of the border. That information may not have been important to Barry but to Jack it was priceless. He had not been told any of that information back in London and so he believed that London didn't know about it. There were also the addresses of safe houses, staged at fifteen mile intervals, between the attack and the border. Fifteen miles was as far as a man on the run could be expected to travel in one night. Jack thought the figure to be a massive exaggeration for a number of reasons. Chief amongst those reasons was the fact that Northern Ireland was so small and so densely populated with police and army. It would not be a problem for them to shut down every major road and a good few minor roads if it came to that. That would make running even a few miles in the dark a very dangerous proposition. Jack got the distinct feeling that the safe houses were nothing more than comfort talk—there to ease any fears that they might have about the operation going south. Regardless, they were set the task of memorising the addresses of all of the safe houses. It was a relatively easy task for Jack , but Fat John did struggle with it—Fat John wasn't much of a thinker.

With the diversions out of the way the training once again shifted to handling the vehicles. Jack would drive a lorry on the day of the attack but he was also given lessons on the council vans as well, just to be safe. They were a fairly relaxed few weeks, but as with all relaxation surrounding the IRA, it was only ever temporary.

"Get a good night's sleep," Barry said on entering Jack's room. "We are on. First thing in the morning."

Jack swallowed hard.

"Where?" Jack asked.

"You will be told once you are on the road," Barry said.

"Who will be travelling with me?"

"You will find out everything that you need to know in the morning. Get your head down. I will ask Father Joe to say a prayer for you."

With that he was gone. As Jack lay on the bed replaying in his head what he would have to do to bring this whole mess to an end and contemplating just how important his success would be to saving the lives of hundreds of innocent people, he thought that he would never get to sleep. He was very wrong. Within half an hour he was completely under and dreaming the dreams of the righteous.

17

Countdown

It was a glorious Irish morning in late summer. It was a time of year that Jack always associated with renewal and rebirth—even more so than the spring. It was hard to put a finger on exactly why he felt that way about that time of year, but he assumed that the feelings were rooted somewhere in his childhood. Like every other child who spent the summer months running wild through the city streets, there was a part of young Jack that never wanted the summer holidays to end. But another part of him knew that it was time to make preparations to return to school, and that part of him looked forward to it, even if he never admitted that. A new school year with a new uniform and new schoolbag and new pens and new pencils. It was a new start; a chance to put right all of the things that had not gone so well the year before—I will listen to the teachers—I will do all of my homework.

As Barry and Jack drove into the border market town of Newry at ten that morning, the back-to-school shoppers were already out in force. Mothers were dragging their less than impressed looking kids around the shops in preparation for the big day. Jack smiled. It was such a perfect scene—so typical, so familiar and so normal. It was a scene that was being played out in towns and cities all over the country. If all went according to plan then none of them would ever know just how close they came to waking up in a new Northern Ireland that was in a state of perpetual war. If it didn't go according to plan then those same children would never know what normality was for at least a couple of generations. That thought weighed heavily on Jack and try as he might he simply couldn't shake the burden of the responsibility. He felt under pressure; he felt nervous; but most of all, he felt alone.

It had been so long since he had last made contact with anyone from the mainland that he sometimes wondered if they had completely given up on him. Perhaps some new voice in the intelligence community had spoken up with a new plan and Jack was not part of that plan. These feelings were only natural but Jack knew better than anyone that such feelings could lead to mistakes, which in turn could lead to him being discovered. He sighed quietly as he searched for composure.

Barry had returned to his former, serious self and he didn't say much during the half hour drive into Newry. In an odd kind of way Jack found this regression in Barry reassuring— at least he wasn't the only one who was feeling pressure at that moment. Hopefully all of the men involved in the attacks would be so caught up in their own personal concerns and worries that they wouldn't notice Jack's.

"Son of a bitch!" Barry yelled as a taxi driver pulled out in front of them. "Christ I could be doing without this bullshit today."

Jack looked at him and nodded. Barry never lost his temper. The stress and strain of what was to come was taking a toll. The suspension of their brown Cortina took a hell of a battering as they drove along the cobbled street which ran along the canal. There was a high red brick wall to their right with the words Fisher & Fisher Fuel Merchants written on it in six foot high, white letters. The wall ran on for several hundred yards with large iron gates punctuating it every 100 yards or so. Dirty signs fixed to the wall yelled of the wares inside—coal; gas; oil, etc. These signs were matched with messages painted with steady hands proclaiming loyalty to the IRA. There was no doubt in the mind of anyone driving through Newry just where the heart and soul of the town lay.

Lorries were queuing to get into the yard and a steady trickle of vehicles was also leaving through the gates. Most were heading back into Newry, which was in Northern Ireland, but a few were making their way into the Republic of Ireland. The town was a hub of activity for the illegal fuel trade and merchants such as Fisher's were told that they were to buy a certain amount of that illegal haul—buy it or watch the business go up in smoke. It was just one more branch of the terrorists' ever growing empire but it was a branch that the authorities seemed powerless to bring under control.

This really was the frontier in the fight against the IRA. They could carry out an attack against the police or army and within minutes they could be across the border and free—the police and army were not allowed to cross into the Republic. Although there was an official policy of co-operation between the security forces in the north and the security forces in the south, the reality was that the Irish police were never likely to arrest any of the fleeing IRA men, and in many cases they actually aided in their escape—if Barry and his comrades had their way that day would mark an end to British non-incursion into the south. The Irish government would protest, but with a couple of helicopters and half a dozen tanks against the industrial might of the British army, there wasn't a hell of a lot that they could do about it. This was what the Irish government really feared in the dirty war—the British would one day return to the south, using the atrocities committed in the north, or on the mainland, as an excuse. The idea had been publically forwarded by more than one senior UK politician in the recent past. Although unlikely, in Ireland no one could ever say never.

"That's a big place," Jack remarked, trying to muster as much enthusiasm as he could. "It seems so out of place in a small country town like Newry. Haven't seen anything like it since I was living in London. Down at the docks."

"Yeah, it used to serve the whole area. Fuel was landed at Warrenpoint and then brought by barge into Newry, along the canal," Barry explained. "These days everything is brought in by truck. The canal is only used for pleasure sailing or fishing these days—and with pollution from the factories, even that is dying out. The coal yard is only holding on by a thread. There was even talk of it being sold to make way for a shopping centre. The whole town is undergoing regeneration and as you drive into town Fishers' yard is the first thing that greets you. Red bricks and coal dust doesn't exactly fit in with what the developers have in mind."

Jack listened intently—it was distracting and comforting to listen to Barry's impromptu history lesson at that moment— some small semblance of normality on a day when normality was at a premium. Although there was a slight hint of regret in Barry's voice he stopped short of condemning outright the redevelopment plans—no doubt the IRA would have their fingers in that pie too once it was out of the planning process. Just one more step up the corporate ladder for Barry and his cronies. With so many successful business interests, both legitimate and those that were anything but, Jack wondered wryly why they didn't just bide their time until they were in a position to buy Northern Ireland back. At the very least there nothing that life in a united Ireland could offer them financially that they didn't already have.

They arrived at the end of the long wall and pulled into the yard through the last gate. There were no lorries waiting at that gate. The gates closed behind them as they pulled into the yard. The part of the yard was isolated from the rest of the large complex. It was a service area used for the yard's own vehicles, but on that morning the vehicles in the service area did not belong to the business. The staff who worked in the service yard had already been dealt with—masked men entered the yard over the wall at 7 am. They lay in wait for the staff to arrive for work. They were instructed to move all of the yard's own vehicles to another part of the complex. Masked men accompanied them on the short trip there and back again. Then one by one, and at gunpoint, the staff were escorted to a wooden hut at the back of the yard to be tied up and gagged. The hut was used to store tyres and batteries and it was dirty and cramped. If any of them broke free from their restraints they could have easily broken free from the flimsy wooden structure. There wasn't a man or woman in that hut who would have dared—when the IRA told you to sit down and shut up, you sat down and shut up. Being tied up was for the most part a convention—the victims expected it and the police expected it and the terrorists were only too happy to meet their expectations—just all part of a larger dance that was played out day in day out all over Northern Ireland.

Jack was completely knocked back by what he saw in the service yard. Every vehicle that was to be used in the bombings was there in that one place. It was not like the IRA to put all of their eggs into one basket. Then again, perhaps that's exactly what they did—the intelligence services hadn't had much luck working out what was typical behaviour for the IRA and in all his time in Ireland Jack had never discovered anything more useful to add to that lack of information. In fact, Jack knew that if the operation came to an end in that yard then there wouldn't be a single piece of useful information that he could take back to London beyond the names of some IRA men and details of one operation. No professional army could claim that level of information security. If anyone called the police to report suspicious activity then the game would be well and truly up. It was yet another sign of just how confident these men were. They could take over part of a business, assemble several massive bombs in one place, and all with the certain knowledge that no one would dare inform on them. They had their own moles in the security forces and when it came to secrecy, they would stop at nothing to protect themselves. In the hearts and minds of the people of Newry they were already part of a united Ireland and it was the security forces that were operating illegally— the terror group's sense of invulnerability was born out of a much deeper sense of entitlement.

The street cleaners were lined up along one side of the yard and the lorries at the other side. Even though the street cleaners had just been re-sprayed, someone had enough good sense to take them out for a dive along a few dirty roads to give them that well used appearance. In addition to the lorries that had been widely discussed in their plans, and which Jack had many opportunities to drive, there was also a lorry piled high with bales of barley straw, as well as a milk float carrying over a dozen milk cans. Jack reckoned that these unfamiliar vehicles were either already in the yard for some reason, and therefore completely incidental, or they were part of the plan to be used to create a diversion or set up a roadblock. If he needed to know why they were there, he would be told.

Jack was just about to leave the car when Barry grabbed him firmly by the arm. Instinctively he tried to shake Barry off.

"What?" Jack snapped.

"One last thing," Barry said.

He reached across to the glove compartment, opened the door and then he slipped out a small pistol.

"A wee present from your uncle Barry. Don't say that I never do anything for you," Barry said.

"Thanks mate," Jack said, with a grin. "Let's hope I don't need it."

They got out of the car and made their way across the oil-splattered, pot holed, yard towards a group of five men. They were casually dressed.

"Great morning, gents," Barry beamed.

The men groaned and nodded in agreement.

"So, are we all set to go?" Barry asked.

"Almost," said Fat John. "The explosives experts are having a fry-up at the Monkey. They should have been here ten minutes ago."

Barry checked his watch.

"Not to worry; I'm sure they will be along soon. We have

lots of time to play with. If you give your vehicles one last check over before they come—oil, water, air; then we will be good to go," said Barry.

Each of them headed to their assigned vehicle. Jack kept his head down as he crossed to his bread lorry. He walked around the lorry checking the tyres before checking the oil and water. Everything was good. He opened the door to the cab on the driver's side. A long grey coat with the logo Baird's Best Breads emblazoned on it was sitting on the seat. He put the coat on. At the very least, he looked the part. He climbed up into the cab and waited. In his head he told himself to pay no heed to the other terrorists—even at that late stage there was still the possibility that he would be rumbled. As he waited the milk float pulled out of the yard. Jack knew that milk floats were notoriously unstable—perhaps they were going to tumble it to close off a particular road?

He distracted himself by looking through the cab. There was a packet of cigarettes sitting on the dashboard and an A to Z tucked into the panel of the driver's door. Apart from the fact that the cab was a little too clean, it was very convincing. With the cab well and truly searched, Jack looked out at the other drivers. John was sitting back in the cab of his council sweeper with his eyes closed. Jack grinned. No doubt he had one or two drinks before he went to bed. Fat John was bobbing up and down in his cab—probably dropped a sweet, or a cigarette, Jack thought. The others were simply sitting impatiently.

Eventually a car pulled into the yard. Like a clown car from a circus; five large men climbed out of the tiny vehicle.

"Jesus Christ," Jack said, under his breath. "Have you ever heard of keeping a low profile?"

Jack only recognised one of the men—Cathal. The men said their goodbyes to one another before heading to their assigned partners. The hairs on Jack's neck stood on end as Cathal moved towards his lorry. He waved at Jack and smiled as he approached. Cathal got into the passenger's side.

"Cathal," Jack said, with as much keenness as he could manage.

"Looks like they have finally let the lads out together," Cathal said, with a grin. His yellowing teeth caught the early morning sunlight, and the sight of them turned Jack's stomach.

"So it would seem," Jack said.

Jack started the lorry.

"So boss; where too?" Jack asked.

"We are going to take the coast road. The others will all take different routes," Cathal said.

Jack looked at him with mild confusion. The coast road had not been mentioned during the planning stages; at least not until after the attacks. Was this yet again Cathal letting him know that they still didn't quite trust him?

"You take a left, then a right, then another right..."

"I know where it is," Jack said.

He started the lorry and pulled out slowly. Two gunmen opened the gates and Jack and Cathal drove out onto the road. Within twenty minutes they had cleared the traffic of Newry and were cruising steadily along the dual carriageway. For a few minutes both men got lost in their own thoughts. For his part Jack was putting in place a plan to stop the attack. He glanced at Cathal. There was every possibility that sometime in the next few hours Jack would have to put a bullet in the old man's head—up close and personal—and he wasn't entirely convinced that he would be able to go through with it.

Cathal was looking out of the side window. It took Jack a few moments to work out what he was doing. His eyes were trained on the side mirror. Every few minutes Cathal checked his watch.

"Are we running late?" Jack asked.

"What?"

"You keep looking at your watch. Are we running late?" he asked again.

"No, but we are on a tight schedule, as you know."

"Surely we have hours yet? It will take less than two hours to get to Lisburn."

"It's not as straightforward as that. We have spotter cars along the route who will report back to the command centre. We will stop every so often and call in to check on any potential problems. That all takes time," explained Cathal.

Jack nodded his head as Cathal spoke. The expression on Jack's face remained stoic but inside he was smiling—he would be able to deal with Cathal when they made one of the stops.

As they neared the port town of Warrenpoint they ran into traffic. From their elevated position high up in the cab of the lorry, Jack could see that the army had set up a checkpoint just before the roundabout.

"Bloody hell," Jack said. "It's the army."

"Calm down. Whatever happens now, happens," Cathal said. "If we turn around it will draw their attention. There is nothing that we can do about it. They only search one in ten vehicles. We will be grand. Get your driver's licence out."

Jack reached into the left pocket of his jeans and he pulled out the forged licence. The Northern Ireland licence had photo I.D. and although it was not a legal requirement to carry it, or even produce it on the spot, the police and army made it very difficult for those who didn't carry it. Jack inched the lorry forwards. On their right stood an old tower house which looked more like a proper Norman castle; the locals even called it Narrow Waters Castle. On the opposite side of the road a nineteenth century gate lodge was the scene of much activity. The milk float from the yard was parked by the aide of the gate lodge and two of the terrorists were offloading the milk cans. The milk float was not a diversion. It was part of the day's attacks. Jack was incredulous—the army was literally fifty yards away from the men. From his vantage point Jack could see at least seven soldiers crouched down along the side of the road with their guns pointing in that general direction.

Two soldiers broke free from the rest of the patrol and they began to make their way towards Jack. One of the soldiers was checking the traffic in the left hand lane, and the other soldier was checking the right hand lane. As they neared the milk float, one of the soldiers moved across to have a look at what they were doing. The solider was holding his gun in a firing position but it was not pointed at the men. The soldier said something to the men as they continued to move the milk cans. He then called to his colleague. The other soldier approached the milk float. They slung they rifles over their backs and then they began helping the terrorists move the milk cans.

"I don't believe it," Jack said, as he watched the scene play out.

"I told you. If you relax, everything will be alright."

"But they are..."

"Whatever you are going to say, don't. Not here. You never know who is listening at checkpoints," Cathal said.

Jack wanted to get out of the lorry and scream at the two young soldiers. Jack assumed the milk cans were packed with explosives. He also assumed that they were being off loaded at the gate house so that they could be picked up later. How could the soldiers not tell that the cans contained solid explosives rather than liquid milk? It stupefied Jack.

The soldiers moved back towards the checkpoint. Jack lowered his window as he approached the checkpoint. Casually Jack inspected the castle on the other side of the carriageway. The castle guarded a waterway which marked the border between the north and the south. There used to be a ferry that sailed every hour from north to south across the waterway but it was attacked and sunk in the early days of the current conflict—the terrorists thought it was hitting the state as it cost a lot to replace the boat; the government were happy not to pay to replace it as it had been used many times in the past as a quick escape route for the IRA following attacks in South Down.

Suddenly there was a burst of activity. The signs letting motorists know there was a checkpoint ahead were removed and the soldiers jumped into the back of their armoured Land Rovers. Jack sighed with relief. As he was winding the window back up Jack noticed something shining high up in the mountain on the other side of the waterway. Then something else blinking sunlight back at him a little further down mountain. The entire scene was obviously being observed. Jack was just about to say as much to Cathal but he stopped himself—as if Cathal didn't already know that they were being watched. That was probably the reason why he was so calm. If the soldiers did open the lorry and find the bomb then the gunmen with sniper rifles on the wooded mountain across the water would provide them with cover. There was probably a getaway car following them too.

Warrentpoint was a small town but it contained one of the largest ports in Ireland. Goods used to be moved by barge after being landed at Warrenpoint, but with the death of canals that distribution role had been taken up by lorries. It was normally a busy town, but with the checkpoint staggering the flow of traffic through the town, it had greatly reduced the time it took them to make it to the other side. Once safely through the town and heading along the picturesque South Down coast, Jack decided he had waited long enough for answers. If Cathal didn't trust him enough to fill him in on some of the last minute details, then he really was of no further use to Jack.

"Why were they taking the milk cans off back there," Jack asked.

"Today is going to go down in Irish history, for better or worse. There were some last minute changes to our plans to gain the maximum impact. The bomb back there is one of those additions," Cathal explained. "It will take place later tonight, just when everyone thinks the worst is over."

"I see. But don't you worry that we are spreading ourselves a bit thin? Too many irons in the fire?" Jack asked.

"In an operation like this, the more irons the more confusion and the more likely we are to get away with it. And besides, after today we will be on lockdown for months, if not years. There was one last bit of business that we needed to get out of the way before that happened."

Jack looked at him with confusion.

"On Bloody Sunday the Brits shot dead unarmed men and children with the knowledge that they could get away with it. They were little more than animals to be hunted. The bastards who carried out those murders will pay for their crimes today. That bomb is meant for the Parachute Regiment. Today is their day of reckoning."

His words left Jack feeling cold. How big was this attack? How many old scores were to be settled on that day?

"That was seven years ago, Cathal," Jack said. "How can you even be sure that you will get them and not some other regiment?"

"And? The passage of time does not impart innocence on them. Just because they have got away with it this long doesn't mean..."

"You misunderstand what I'm trying to say," Jack interrupted. "How many of the original soldiers from Derry in 1972 do you think will be active today? Many of them will have moved on by now, don't you think?"

"Aye, but the symbolism is the thing that matters. We were never told the names of any of the soldiers who carried out the Bloody Sunday attacks. The only thing that we could focus our hatred on was the regiment itself. By the end of today we will know the names of many of them as they are read out on the news. They came here to kill us and we simply can't let that challenge go unanswered."

"I suppose," Jack conceded.

As they made their way along the narrow coastal road Jack felt really uneasy. Stopping one attack was going to be hard enough, but trying to stop all of the attacks was something that he could not possible achieve on his own. The next three towns that they would pass through all had police stations. If he pulled into one of those stations and turned his gun on Cathal then he could wash his hands off the entire affair. The only problem was that once Cathal and the others were in custody they would clam up completely. He had already learned about the bomb outside Warrenpoint; if he held on for a while he might learn more. There would be other opportunities to turn Cathal in as they got closer to the target.

Cathal began to play with the radio.

"How do you turn the damn wireless on?" Cathal snapped.

Jack reached over and pushed the volume button. The radio came to life.

"More on that story at the top of the hour. You are listening to Radio Ulster."

There was a long pause before the beeps signalling the run-up to the eleven o' clock news played over the speakers.

"Monday, 27th August. This is Radio Ulster. Today's top stories and there is only one story dominating the news agenda. Police in the Irish Republic have confirmed that Lord Louis Mountbatten, last Viceroy of India and the Queen's cousin, has been killed in a massive explosion on his boat, Shadow V. An intensive search and rescue operation is underway off the coast of Mullaghmore, County Sligo, and it is feared that there are multiple fatalities. News of the attack has only been released in the last hour and there has been no comment so far from Buckingham Palace. For more, we cross to our Dublin correspondent Jackie Doyle."

"Bloody hell," Jack gasped. "Mountbatten?"

Cathal grinned.

"This is only the start. By the time the bomb outside Warrenpoint goes off tonight, just before midnight, the Brits will know exactly who it is they have been messing with all these years. This is our day."

"Did you know about Mountbatten?" Jack asked.

"You know better than to ask me that question."

"For fucks sake. I have done everything that you have asked me to do without question. Now I'm heading into the heart of a storm. Is it so hard for you to give me straight answer?" Jack snapped.

"For now you already know everything that you need to know. Tomorrow I will answer any questions that you might have," Cathal said, firmly.

Jack sat back in the seat, seething with quiet rage. He was looking out of the window but his eyes were not really on the road.

"There have been a couple of last minute changes to the plan," Cathal announced. "You were originally going to be picked up by a fishing boat outside the village of Annalong and then taken to a container ship off the coast. We have had to move the pickup point to Kilkeel, which is a little further along the coast. There was a riot in Annalong last night and the police are still out in force."

As they arrived at the tourist hotspot of Newcastle, County Down, Cathal gave Jack street by street instructions on where to go. Jack followed the instructions to the letter. As they left the town and drove off into the countryside, Jack had no idea that he was being directed away from Lisburn, the main target of the attack.

18

The Best Laid Plans

Jack had done his very best to learn all that he could about the area before they set out that day, but none of that research, no matter how rigorous, could in any way compare to the local knowledge and understanding that Cathal possessed. That simple fact put Jack at more of a disadvantage than he knew, and it was that lack of local knowledge that was leading Jack away from where he was supposed to be going without him even knowing about it.

"We need to stop up here," Cathal said, pointing to a petrol station. "I have to make a couple of phone calls to make sure the road ahead is clear."

Jack did not respond. He carefully pulled the lorry off the main road onto the forecourt of the Shell station. Out of habit he checked the fuel level. The gauge indicated that the tank was still over half full. Cathal jumped out of the cab and he made his way inside.

As the countdown raced on Jack knew that whatever he was going to do to put an end to the bombs, he would have to do it soon. He slipped his hand into his pocket and squeezed the gun in a futile act of reassurance. With the others Jack had a fair idea how they would react with a gun pointed to their head—none of them were martyrs—their training had taught them not to sacrifice themselves. Cathal was different. He was old school IRA from a time when the expectation was that they would never come out on top in a direct fight against the British. It was a time when being caught brought with it an automatic death sentence. Jack simply didn't know how he would react, but he had a terrible feeling that once Jack revealed himself to Cathal then one of them was going to die.

From a purely practical standpoint he would have to turn on Cathal before they reached the target. The others could already be there, all armed and all watching for trouble. If a fight broke out Jack wouldn't stand a chance and innocent bystanders could be caught up in the crossfire. There was also the possibility that the bombs had been fitted with remote control detonators as a back-up to the timers—if Cathal had anything to do with the preparation of the devices then that redundancy would surely be there.

Cathal returned to the lorry and got in.

"The news is filled with reports on Mountbatten," Cathal said, with quiet pride. "There all kinds of experts lining up to give their opinion on what happened. Messages of sympathy are coming in from all over the world. It could not have worked out any better."

"They will be talking about it for years to come," Jack said.

"They surely will," Cathal agreed.

Cathal turned the radio on as they pulled out of the forecourt onto the road.

"...Bradbury Place, Castle Street and the North Circular Road are closed due to suspicions devices. So far six devices have exploded and three more have been destroyed by the Army in controlled explosions. An unofficial police source has told Radio Ulster that the bombs and bomb alerts have effectively put the city of Belfast into lockdown. No one had been seriously hurt in any of the alerts but both the Royal and City hospital have been put on a heightened state of readiness should the situation deteriorate."

Jack glanced round at Cathal expecting to see him wearing a smile. He didn't even look content.

"How did the phone calls go?" Jack asked.

"Grand. The roads ahead are clear. The diversions in Belfast are working, as you can hear," Cathal said.

There was something about Cathal's tone that made Jack feel uneasy.

"Something wrong?" Jack asked.

"Nothing that we can't deal with. We anticipated that more of the soldiers from the base would be involved with the bombs in Belfast. Some of the volunteers from the city are rallying local support. They are taking to the streets. A bit of civil unrest should flush a few more out of the base."

"Aww," Jack said, simply.

"Not a big problem, but it will put the main attack off by about an hour," Cathal explained.

Jack looked at him with alarm.

"What, do you suggest that we just drive around with a lorry loaded with explosives until it is more convenient?" Jack asked.

"You really do worry too much. We are going to pull into an empty farmhouse that belongs to one of our volunteers. It's just down the road a bit on this side of Castlewellen. We can go inside and make a nice cup of tea. Maybe that will help steady your nerves?"

"I am not nervous, but the longer we are driving around with this bomb the more chance there is that we will get caught. Does the volunteer know that we are coming?"

"Relax. This has all been planned weeks ago. We have back up plans in place for every conceivable eventuality."

Jack smiled.

"What's funny?" Cathal asked.

"You say that you have planned for every eventuality. I sure as hell hope so."

Cathal grinned.

"It's the next laneway on the left," Cathal instructed.

Jack applied the brakes and then slowly pulled the lorry off the main road into the laneway. The suspension rocked the vehicle like a boat when he slammed on the brakes.

"What the hell is it now?" Cathal snapped.

"We will never get this thing down that lane," Jack replied, exasperated.

"Sure you will, man. Take her nice and slowly and you will be grand. If you take the odd stone out of the walls, they can be fixed," Cathal said.

The walls lining the lane were rather fragile looking, dry stone. The bramble and whins indicated that it was not well travelled by either heavy machinery or by livestock. Jack did his best to negotiate the narrow passage, with the fragility of his cargo in the back of his mind at all times. Eventually they reached a yard surrounded by derelict farm buildings.

"Looks like that cup of tea is out," Jack remarked, with a smirk.

Cathal reached under his seat. Watching him carefully, Jack slipped a hand into his pocket and grasped his gun. His grip relaxed when Cathal produced a denim bag.

"Good boy scouts and IRA men," Cathal said, patting the bag. "We may as well find a seat inside. It will be a while before we hit the road again."

As they got out of the cab Jack had a feeling that this episode in his life, this relationship in particular, was fast coming to an end. He got a sense that Cathal was holding something from him and that unplanned tea break was nothing more than a rouse to keep him busy.

Cathal walked round to the back of the main farmhouse with Jack following close behind. The door was locked. Cathal threw his shoulder against the door and it yielded with ease. They went inside. Jack had been expecting a dirty, run-down wreck. What greeted him was rustic and homely. They sat down by the Formica covered table and Cathal poured each of them a cup of tea from a thermos. Jack sipped on the unsweetened tea. It tasted bitter. It was a common mistake, Jack mused—putting the teabags in when filling the thermos. Cathal's face did not register the slightest trace of disgust as he drank his tea. Cathal looked at his watch.

"It is almost two," he announced. "We will stay here until three thirty and then hit the road."

"The bombings in Belfast are already underway. If we leave it too long do we not run the risk of wasting all that cover?"

Cathal took out a cigarette and lit it. He offered Jack one. Jack refused.

"It's not like you to turn down a smoke. Go on, it will help you relax," Cathal insisted.

"I'm fine, thanks. I am trying to cut down."

"You are a hard man to get a read on," Cathal continued. "One minute you are all tense and worried, and the next minute you are cool as cucumber. Me, I like to steer the middle road all of the time. It helps me to keep my wits about me, but at the same time it allows me to do the kind of things that need to be done in order to win this war."

He sucked on his cigarette for a few moments.

"Do you know what bothers me about you?" Cathal asked.

Jack paused for a moment.

"I ask too many questions?" Jack replied.

"No, funny enough the opposite is true. All of the other men in the team have taken me to one side over the last few weeks and they have pumped me for information. Barry has been the worst. Come on Cathal, you have known me all my life," Cathal added, in a mocking voice. "But not you. I give you an answer and you accept it. For the most part. In fact, until today I can't recall you ever questioning anything that I have told you."

"And you have a problem with that?" Jack asked, with confusion.

Cathal leaned forwards across the table.

"As a matter of fact, I do. You are an intelligent man. The other arseholes have been drawing maps on scraps of paper, even though they were instructed not to. God help them, they are just not clever enough to remember details like that. As for military strategy. Forget about it. Not like you. You are always thinking ahead. You are always analysing the situation. They have nothing on you."

"When it is your life on the line, Cathal, a wee bit of thought is hardly a crime," Jack protested.

"True. But only a wee bit of thought."

Jack stood up.

"I don't know where you are going with this Cathal, but I think I have heard just about enough of your random bullshit."

"Sit down lad. I haven't quite finished," Cathal instructed.

Jack did as he was asked.

"I am not entirely convinced that you have been one hundred percent honest with us," Cathal said. "I can't be sure what it is that you are hiding, and it could be something very innocent, like a woman or a drinking problem, but there is something. That is why we won't be going to Lisburn."

"What the hell!" Jack snapped. "After all that training. All that bullshit over the last few weeks. Now you want to pull me from the attack?"

"No, I said you were not going to Lisburn. I appreciate that you want to do this. That you want to strike a blow to the state that killed your mother, and I fully intend to give you that opportunity, just not in Lisburn."

"I don't understand," Jack said.

"We are going to take our bomb to Banbridge. It is a similar set-up to Lisburn. Mainly Protestant town and home to many families with connections to the security forces. Our bomb will be the last distraction before the big attack in Lisburn. Our bomb explodes at four, and the attack in Lisburn takes place at four thirty."

"That's grand," Jack said. "I do not have a problem with that."

"Good lad. I had a feeling that you would understand."

"What is that supposed to mean?" Jack asked.

Cathal jumped to his feet and then slammed his hands down hard on the table.

"A real IRA man would never simply accept an accusation

like that," Cathal growled. "A real IRA man would have drawn out and left me lying on my arse in a heap!"

Jack stood up slowly and then he leant in towards Cathal.

"Push me any further, old man, and I will leave you lying in a heap," Jack said.

Cathal smiled.

"That's more like it. That's more convincing," Cathal said.

"You still don't believe me?"

"I am afraid not," Cathal added.

"I don't understand. Why did you let me take part in the operation if you don't believe me? Why not kill me before now?"

Cathal smiled, then let slip a little chuckle.

"Because we needed you. The British needed to know that they had a man on the inside. If they didn't have a man on the inside do you think we would have been able to take that lorry through the checkpoint? Those soldiers were ordered to let you pass. Your own side have been following you every step of the way and that is why we have been able to put the real bombs in place. The plan is the same, only with my plan the security forces will be following empty lorries and council sweepers to the four corners of Northern Ireland."

"Bullshit," Jack snapped. "I saw the bomb back at the yard when I was checking the lorry. You are full of shit!"

Cathal stared at Jack with hatred spread across his face like a mask. Suddenly his mood changed to euphoria.

"Christ almighty, you are easy," Cathal sniggered.

"You bastard," Jack fired back.

Jack sat down at the table. Cathal paced the room, smiling to himself. For a short time nothing more was said. Cathal sat down.

"I knew that you were on the level," Cathal said.

"Aye? How could you be so sure?"

"Two things. One of the sweepers was intercepted shortly after it left Newry."

"And the other?"

"You would have pulled the gun on me that Barry gave to you if you thought you had been compromised."

Jack smiled. Cathal got up and moved to the sink to rinse out his cup.

"So the attack goes ahead? According to plan?" Jack asked.

"Yeah. But we are going to set our bomb off in Banbridge. Even with two devices out of the picture, Lisburn should still create one hell of a bang."

Cathal turned around to face Jack. Jack was pointing the gun at him.

"That's all that I needed to know," Jack said.

19

Firestorm

The look on Cathal's face was an odd mixture of confusion and disbelief.

"What the hell is this?" Cathal asked.

"This is the end of the road, old man. This is the bit where the evil Brit stops you from murdering men, women and children."

Cathal started laughing again.

"This is not a joke. I am a British agent. You are under arrest."

Cathal lit another cigarette.

"You know, I pushed for them to kick you off this operation. I begged them to set you up. No one would listen to me."

"So how did you know who I was," Jack scoffed.

"From that first night in the bar."

"And how could you have been so sure?"

"Your mother, or the woman who you said was your mother. I knew her better than I said. In fact, if you were who you said you were, then there is a very real possibility that you would be my son, if you know what I mean? You are no son of mine."

"Thank God for that."

"So, are you going to tell me who you really are?"

"Are you going to tell me all of the plans for today?"

"Fair point lad, fair point."

Another long draw on his cigarette.

"There were too many people in the movement who

wanted you to be on the level; that was the problem. I was nothing but a paranoid old fool."

"Stop it, mate. You'll make me cry."

"OK, I'll let it go. The regrets of an old volunteer. But there was one thing that they did let me get my own way on."

"Yes?"

"Your gun. Barry loaded it with blanks."

Without pausing Jack called his bluff as he aimed to Cathal's right and he started firing. Debris flew everywhere as round after round went off. Cathal stood up and shook his head.

"Seems like they didn't even let me have my own way with that one either."

"So it would seem."

"So, what now?"

"Now we go outside, defuse the bomb in the back of the lorry, and then drive to the closest police station to call the attack in."

Cathal started walking towards the kitchen door.

"Whoe, where do you think you are going?"

"To drive the lorry to Banbridge. I would ask you but... Well, you know how it is?"

Jack fired another shot into the wall next to Cathal.

"Cathal, it is over. You always told us to stay alive."

"What I said only applied to brave volunteers of the IRA, not to some lying British bastard and some stupid old man."

He moved again. Another shot exploded the plaster next to Cathal's head.

"I am serious. The next shot will enter your body. Do not move another inch."

Cathal turned to Jack and smiled.

"I may be an old man, but I can still count. You, my old son, are clean out of bullets."

Cathal removed his hand from his coat. He was holding a revolver.

"And I have six."

Jack squeezed the trigger. Click. Then again. Click. Jack grimaced as he waited for the inevitable.

"You don't often get this from the IRA, but I'm going to give you a choice," Cathal said. "You can either drive the lorry for me or I can kill you now and drive it myself."

"Kill me now or kill me later?"

"That's all I have I'm afraid."

"In that case, I'll take later."

"Good lad. Now take a wee seat and we can both sit quietly and think about what we have done for a while. I'm not going to tell you anything in case you are rescued. You are not going to tell me anything useful because you are a lying British bastard."

Stung by the turnaround, Jack sat quietly and waited. He was determined not to give in but in part conceded that if lives were to be saved on that day it would be down to others.

Two hours later they were on the road again. Jack behind the wheel, Cathal watching his every move with the gun trained on him. The look on Cathal's face was one of anger, of contempt, of hatred. Jack didn't even bother trying to engage him in conversation. He knew that he would have one chance to end this, he just didn't know when that chance would come or what it would look like. As they continued along the road the road signs counted down the distance to their target like a stuttering clock—10 miles; 6 miles; 2 miles.

As they pulled off the country road they had been journeying along onto the short stretch of dual carriageway that led into the town of Banbridge, Jack's opportunity presented itself. Ahead of them was another army checkpoint. There was nothing between the lorry and the soldiers except for less than a mile of empty road. Instinctively Jack slowed the lorry.

"What are you doing?" Cathal asked.

"I don't know! What do you want me to do? Turn around? Drive on? What?"

All of the confidence drained from the old man's face. At the last check point there were other vehicles to provide cover, this time around they were alone.

"Drive on," Cathal instructed.

"You are the boss."

Jack applied pressure to the accelerator and he worked his way up the gears. He kept his foot on the accelerator. One way or the other, that lorry was never going to make it past the checkpoint. 500 yards, 400 yards, 300, yards...

"What the hell are you doing!" Cathal yelled.

"I would be more concerned by what they are doing," Jack said, as he nodded towards the men at the checkpoint.

Four of the soldiers were aiming their weapons at the lorry. Cathal looked out of the front window with horror. That was Jack's moment. He slipped the lorry out of gear, opened the door and rolled out. His head made a sickening cracking sound as it hit the ground. As consciousness faded Jack could hear the sound of automatic gunfire. Everything went black.

Jack had no idea how long he had been out, but it was long enough for an ambulance to arrive and for the soldiers to receive instructions from London not to hurt him. That simple message was enough for them to know that Jack was one of their own. Army and police vehicles were surrounding him. Three high sided troop carriers were parked around him providing an effect screen from any prying eyes as the medical team worked on him.

Lisburn! The recollection hit him like a low fast punch to the gut. Jack sat up straight on the stretcher. The pain tormenting his body was subdued by a sudden surge of adrenalin.

"They are going to attack Lisburn," Jack yelled.

One of the soldiers walked over to him.

"Sir, we have intercepted the devices and arrested those involved. The bomb squad is dealing with them at this moment. We were unable to stop the attack at Warrenpoint. There are six dead. Still, it could have been a lot worse. Your passenger was shot several times. He passed a few minutes ago. All he said was that we were too late."

Jack lay back. His head hurt and he was exhausted. Six dead, he thought. If only he could have stayed conscious for a few more minutes. He thought he had more time. Cathal told him he had more time. Cathal, for the last time, had lied. Regret soon passed as his mind turned to thoughts of home. As the medics continued to treat him, Jack closed his eyes. He was listening to the conversations that were going on around him, but he wasn't taking much in. Eventually his brain did pick up on something. What they were saying didn't make sense. He sat up again and turned to the medic.

"Warrenpoint," Jack began. "What did you say about the bomb at Warrenpoint?"

"It exploded about half an hour ago as a military convoy was driving past. Several vehicles were destroyed, including the lorry containing the device."

"No," Jack protested. "The bomb isn't in a lorry."

The soldier looked confused.

"Sir, it has been confirmed several times. We believe it was in a lorry carrying hay or straw."

Jack lay down again to process the information. His mind took him back to the yard that morning. He sat up again.

"What about the bomb in the milk cans at the gatehouse?"

"Sir?"

"They planted a bomb in the gatehouse."

"Are you sure?"

"Yes. I saw them doing it."

The solider looked with grave concern at one of his comrades.

"What is it," Jack asked.

"The units on the ground are using the gatehouse as the Incident Command Point."

Jack climbed onto his feet.

"Get me the CO in Warrentpoint," he said.

The soldier talked into his radio for a few moments before handing it to Jack. A crackly voice came across the device.

"This is Colonel Blair."

"You have to get out of there now. There is a second bomb in the gatehouse."

"Are you sure? We have searched the area and found nothing."

"The milk cans."

There were some incomprehensible orders shouted in the background.

"Colonel Blair?" Jack said.

"We are moving out..."

There was a large burst of static, followed by silence. Jack dropped the radio.

For the second time, he had failed.

After a full assessment it was decided that Jack's injuries were not that extensive. Unless they had been life threatening they would never risk sending him to one of the public hospitals. In a strange way Jack was looking forward to going to one of the army bases for a bit of rest before he went back home. He had been moved to the back of a military ambulance with a single medic. The doors to the ambulance opened and a man in a suit got in.

"Give us a minute, private," said the man.

The soldier got out and closed the door behind him.

"Jack, from what we can tell, your cover is still in place," the man said. "You have been our most successful asset in Ireland in a long time."

Jack looked away. He didn't need to mention how the men killed at Warrenpoint might have a different view on that.

"By following you we were able to intercept all of the devices destined for Lisburn. You saved hundreds of lives today. The only device that we were not able to follow was the one you were driving. Thanks to you, it too was eliminated."

The words were well meaning but they did little to ease the deep sense of loss that he was feeling.

"I know that you have been through a lot but we would like you to continue in this role for a little while longer. They plan to take you out of the country. We have arranged it so that a few of the other bombers have escaped. We would like you to continue with the operation, as planned, and escape with them. We believe they are going to meet with an arms dealer. If we ever hope to end this war we need to cut off their supply of weapons. The majority of that supply chain remains hidden to us. Do you feel up to it?"

Jack was tired. He was sore. He was in mourning for the men that he could not save. The only thing in the world that appealed to him at that moment was the thought of being back home in Scotland, with his family and friends. When this all started it was little more than a well paid job and financial security for his family whether he lived or died. A lot had changed in the years since he first signed up. He was a different man. He felt the burden of his responsibilities keenly. But he was only a man at the end of the day. A sore and beaten man at that.

"What do you say Jack?"

There was a pause.

"How many?" Jack asked. "How many died at Warrenpoint?"

"Seventeen soldiers so far. There was a fire-fight after the attack. We may have killed one of the terrorists."

Jack closed his eyes. This was not an automatic decision, but it was a time sensitive decision. The war would go on with or without him. People would live or die, with or without him. They were asking too much of him.

"We need an answer now, Jack."

Jack looked the man right in the eye. He cleared his throat.

"I..."

THE END